Jeremiah Asher

An autobiography with details of a visit to England

Jeremiah Asher

An autobiography with details of a visit to England

ISBN/EAN: 9783337121044

Printed in Europe, USA, Canada, Australia, Japan

Cover: Foto ©Raphael Reischuk / pixelio.de

More available books at **www.hansebooks.com**

AN AUTOBIOGRAPHY,

WITH

DETAILS OF A VISIT TO ENGLAND,

AND

SOME ACCOUNT OF THE HISTORY OF THE MEETING STREET
BAPTIST CHURCH, PROVIDENCE, R. I., AND OF
THE SHILOH BAPTIST CHURCH, PHILA-
DELPHIA, PA.

BY

REV. JEREMIAH ASHER,

WITH

AN INTRODUCTION

BY

REV. J. WHEATON SMITH.

" Mislike me not for my complexion,
    The shadowed livery of the burning sun,'

PHILADELPHIA
PUBLISHED BY THE AUTHOR.
1862.

PREFACE.

THIS little book goes forth into the world making a humble bow, but no apology. During the past few years, I have been frequently requested by friends, and many of the members of the church with whom it has been my privilege to labor for twelve years, to give some account of my birth, parentage, conversion, call to the ministry, and labors up to the present time. After taking counsel of valued brethren in whose judgment I confide, and prayerfully considering my duty, I have yielded to the request of my friends, and now present my plain, unvarnished tale. I offer nothing but a simple narrative of facts, which, divested though they may be of stirring and romantic incident, I trust may, under the blessing of God, encourage many who, without education, may be called to the work of the Gospel ministry. If this book shall aid any such, and help them to overcome the difficulties and em-barrassments with which they may be called to meet, I shall feel not only that I am amply compensated for my labor, but that I have done some good service to the cause of my Master.

The following sketch of my life is written in humble dependence on God. I have endeavored to relate nothing but facts, and have been guided, I trust, in every line, by the spirit of the truth. With regard to individuals, I have, "nothing extenuated, nor set down aught in malice."

Praying that the great Head of the Church will deign to bless this my humble and unpretending child for the advancement of His own glory, I send it forth into the church and the world. ·   J. A.

PHILADELPHIA, 1862.

CONTENTS.

(v)

CHAPTER VI.

CHAPTER VII.

CHAPTER VIII.

CHAPTER IX.

CHAPTER X.

CHAPTER XI.

CHAPTER XII.

viii

CHAPTER XX.

CHAPTER XXI.

CHAPTER XXII.

CHAPTER XXIII.

CHAPTER XXIV.

INTRODUCTION.

In introducing this little volume to the public, I am influenced partly by a desire to aid its author in the good work to which he is devoting his energies, as the pastor of the Shiloh Baptist Church in Philadelphia—a work in which his labors are arduous, his success ample, but his compensation small. If by any means this trial of authorship should result in his pecuniary profit, by placing in the hands of his brethren a readable and useful book in exchange for what might aid him in the further prosecution of his labors, I should regard the enterprise as not only justifiable, but commendable.

But I am also influenced by the belief that the work has merit. As the story of a Christian life, it enters into Christian experience; and all such experience has value. As a narrative of the early relations existing between our colored brethren and the churches to which they belonged, it presents some interesting facts, which are highly suggestive in their bearing upon these times.   It has also some reminiscences of a still earlier date, lending additional testimony to the historical fact that some of the bravest and most steadfast of our soldiers in the time of onr Revolutionary struggle were men of African descent.   These heroes of a sabler hue have not been honored as their memory deserves, or their children protected in the equal enjoyment of privileges which the fathers fought to secure. It is this thought mainly which induces me to ask a welcome for this little volume, as a contribution to literature from one of that people whose wrongs are many, and whose privileges are few.   J. W. S.

AN AUTOBIOGRAPHY.

CHAPTER I.

BIRTH—PARENTAGE — CAPTURE OF MY GRANDFATHER—
TREATMENT ON BOARD OF HIS VESSEL—THE AMERI-
CAN REVOLUTION—DEATH OF MY GRANDFATHER.

I WAS born in the town of North Branford
County of New Haven, State of Connecticut, on
the 13th of October, 1812. My father's name
was Ruel Asher. He was born in the same
place. His father was stolen from the Coast of
Africa, when about four years of age,—brought
to East Guilford, (now called Madison,) and sold to
Linus Bishop, a ship carpenter, for $200. He
gave him the name of Gad Asher.

My mother, Jerusha Asher, is of the Indian
extraction, and was born in Hartford. She is
now about eighty years of age, and being, therefore, unable to provide for herself, is entirely

1

dependent upon a portion of my slender means
for her support. My father died about seven
years since, aged nearly seventy. My grandfather
had been dead about sixteen years. He fell asleep
in Jesus, after having been a member of the Presbyterian Church for forty years. My eldest sister
(Maria) early embraced a hope in Christ, and united with the Presbyterian Church in New Haven,
under the Pastorate of Rev. S. S. Jocelyn, and for
some eight or ten years lived a worthy member of
that church. It has been my privilege seldom to
meet with one more devoted and heavenly-minded.

I have often listened with feelings of unmingled
grief when my grandfather related the story of
his capture,—stolen away as he was, from father,
mother, brother and sister, never more to see
them, and hurried on board of a slaver, to be
consigned to perpetual bondage.

His father cultivated a portion of land some
distance from his dwelling, which he supposes
produced rice; although he cannot be certain, on
account of his being so young. The mode of
cultivation is not very peculiar. The seed being
sown broadcast upon the land, it is then made the
employment of small children to watch for a sea-

son and prevent the depredations of the feathered tribe.

This department of labor fell to a brother of my grandfather, whom he supposes was some ten or twelve years of age, and whom he was accustomed to take with him for company. One day, whilst thus engaged, he saw two white men coming out of the bush and making towards them, which aroused his suspicions. Therefore, he determined to take his little brother and flee for their lives. The white men immediately gave chase. My grandfather says that it was some time before his brother could make him sensible of his danger. He says that he took hold of him and turned him around, so that he might see his pursuers. Then he became so alarmed that he ran as fast and as long as he could, when at last failing in strength, he gave out. Then his brother took him up on his back, and continued to make all possible speed; but finding their pursuers were gaining upon them so fast, he was obliged to give him up and escape for his own life.

The men-stealers soon reached my grandfather, gagged him, and took him up and put him on board the vessel, when they attempted to comfort him by telling him that they were going to take him home.

The brother made his escape to bear the melancholy tidings to his heart-stricken parents, that their darling little boy was stolen, and they would see him no more.

It was twilight when they brought him on board. He saw that, although a large number of men, women and children who had been also thus stolen, he did not recognize one of them. He was, therefore, very lonely and distressed. They took great pains to quiet him, taking him into the cabin, where they were unusually attentive to him, lest they should lose him; and having no relative or companion on board, he was exempted from many of the horrors of the "middle passage."

This happened about twenty-five or thirty years previous to the American Revolution, when Bishop, who had purchased him, was drafted to go into the service of his country; but preferring the comforts of home to the dangers and hardships of a campaign, he made an offer to his servant Gad of his freedom, upon the condition that he would take his place and serve during the war; to which he readily consented.

He fought side by side with white men in two

or three important battles of the American Revolution, including the memorable battle of Bunker Hill, where he lost his eyesight, which he never regained. He died at the age of nearly one hundred years, nearly seventy years after the termination of the Revolutionary War. After returning to his master, he was required to purchase himself for $200, his original cost, the Continental money which he had received for his services being refused.

There were in the town where Gad Asher resided two other colored soldiers of the Revolution, who were frequently accustomed to talk over the motives which prompted them to "endure hardness." They were the only men that I knew (and I was acquainted with nearly every man in the town) that fought in the terrible and never-to-be-forgotten battle for American Liberty. I was so accustomed to hear these men talk, until I almost fancied to myself that I had more rights than any white man in the town. Such were the lessons taught me by the old black soldiers of the American Revolution. Thus, my first ideas of the right of the colored man to life, liberty and the pursuit of happiness, were received from those old veterans and champions for liberty.

I confess that the result of their teachings gave my parents much trouble ; for whenever I was insulted, I would always resist it. Neither my father nor mother could persuade me that white boys were allowed to insult me because I was colored. I invariably felt justified in defending myself.

CHAPTER II.

RELIGIOUS CONCERN—MY FATHER'S SUSPICIONS AND THREATS—CONTINUED DISTRESS—THOUGHTS OF APOSTACY—FIRST BAPTIST PREACHING AND FIRST BAPTISM AT NORTH BRANFORD.

So far back as I can remember, I have been the subject of religious impressions. When not more than seven or eight years of age, my mind was frequently deeply affected. Thoughts on death and the judgment sometimes completely overwhelmed me, fearing as I did, that I might die in my sins. All this was occasioned principally by reading the Holy Scriptures, which I commenced at a very early age. Before I was twelve years old, I remember to have read the entire New Testament four or five times and the Old Testament with the Apocrypha once and partly through again. More than this, the books of the Apocrypha being favorites with me, I read them the more frequently.

When about twelve or thirteen years of age, I was hired out at the rate of six cents per day in the spring and autumn, and from twelve to eighteen cents in the summer. I was expected to perform at least the half of a man's work. It was at this age that it pleased the Lord to call me from nature's darkness into His own marvellous light. It was in this wise: Upon a certain day of the month of March, my father sent me on an errand, giving me special injunctions to hasten back. Hitherto I had been exceedingly disobedient and dilatory, being easily detained by the many objects which readily attracted my attention. On this occasion, however, I started from home with a full determination to obey my father and follow his instructions—to be blind to all I might see and deaf to all I might hear. Having proceeded about midway, I bethought me of the residence near at hand of an intimate friend, who had become the subject of a late revival of religion, but whom I had not seen since his conversion. It was not, however, on this account that I desired to see him. I had forgotten that he was a changed man. Otherwise, nothing would have induced me to have gone near him, feeling as I did at the time, actually afraid of professing Christians, lest they should address me on the subject of religion. Conversation on this subject always made me feel unhappy, as I fully realized that I was a sinner, living without God and without hope.

The morning was delightful. Every piece of nature appeared to wear a cheerful aspect. My own heart was merry until I looked upon my friend, when the thought of his conversion, together with observing a change in his personal appearance, confused and perplexed me so much, that I was literally speechless. It appeared to me as if his face shone with an unnatural brightness. When, however, he addressed me, all sunshine seemed to depart. His very first words pierced my heart, convicting me of my disobedience to my parents and showing me my utter sinfulness before God.

I was unhappy, feeling myself to be a condemned sinner in the sight of God. As he interrogated me concerning my confusion, I was unwillingly forced to confess that I was unwell; when he took occasion to speak to me of the mercy of God, the love of the Lord Jesus Christ in dying for sinners, and my duty to repent of my sins. Such were his words and so earnestly were they spoken, that they went as arrows to my soul, and made me as a wounded bird.

Leaving my friend and walking onwards, I resolved to amend my ways, and no more to disobey my parents. I therefore hastened my pace and soon arrived at home again, thereby pleasing my father. Observing that I was sad at heart, he spoke kindly to me, and for the remainder of the day exacted very little from me.

Night came; but, oh, what a night! To me it was one of densest darkness. I could obtain no sleep to my eyes nor slumber to my eyelids. I was afraid to sleep, feeling that such a sinner as I was, deserved to be turned into hell. I could not as yet see any way of escape, as I remembered the Scripture: "The soul that sinneth, it shall die." I felt, too, that my condemnation was just, so that I could not hope to be forgiven.

The morning came,—then noon-day; but as yet no relief. Dark as night was, I wished for its return, as it appeared to me as if every body regarded me as I viewed myself.

My father, notwithstanding his skepticism about religious matters, very soon appeared to understand or suspect the cause of my trouble, and declared himself to be determined to relieve me from what he termed my gloomy feelings. He inquired of me if I was "serious." To which making no reply, he bade me go to work, giving me a double task, which he insisted should be performed before the sun went down, and at the same time threatening me, that should he see me troubling myself any more on the subject of religion, he would punish me very severely.

Distressed in my mind, I went to my work, but continued many days thereafter in trouble, as I could not understand how God could be just, and yet the Justifier of the ungodly. At length I was brought to see the blood of Christ cleanseth from all sin, and to seek forgiveness through His merits. I soon saw in Christ (a miserable condemned sinner though I felt myself to be,) all that I needed; and being set before me in the Scriptures as suffering and dying for me, and then rising again for my justification, He seemed to me as "the chiefest among ten thousand and altogether lovely."

It then seemed to me as if my sins were really many more and worse than they had been, but I felt as though there were more than sufficient in Jesus to atone for them all. Then I experienced an inward joy, to which I had hitherto been a stranger. I felt assured of my part in the Saviour, and trust, that to the latest day of my life, to hope for acceptance with God only through the merits of a crucified Saviour.

During the whole of this time I do not remember to have heard a sermon, attended a prayer-meeting, or engaged in any religious conversation, until it pleased the Lord, by His Holy Spirit, to bring me to trust in His dear Son alone for salvation, for which I praise His holy name. That day I not only felt joy, comfort and peace, but I also experienced an unusual degree of strength. My task was soon performed, and I retired to meditate upon the goodness of God and thank Him for what He had done for my poor soul.

I continued in this way for some length of time; but having no one to guide and instruct me, I was soon led away by the temptations which surrounded me on every hand; and, although I made no pretentions to religion, I ever after revered and respected those who loved the Saviour, yet I seldom, if ever, spoke to any one on the subject. At length I began to think it was all a delusion, and endeavored to give it up and live in and enjoy the world. I thought that I was too young to give my attention to the consideration of the subject of religion. Although I always delighted to visit the house of the Lord and loved the place where

His honor dwelleth, such was seldom my privilege.

About this time, there came to North Branford a Baptist minister, the first one that I ever heard of since John the Baptist. I did not know that such people upon the face of the earth, holding the views, doctrines, principles and practices as the Baptist denomination, existed. He seemed as though he would "turn the place upside-down," —not because of his fame as a preacher, but for the reason that he declared that baptism could only be rightly performed by immersion. He preached in a small school-house, to which the people flocked from all quarters to hear him. The Lord worked with him, and a number of the most wicked and profligate young men in the town were converted. One entire family, which consisted, I think, of eight members, were announced to put on the Lord Jesus Christ by being immersed in the name of the Father, Son, and Holy Spirit. This was to take place on the Sabbath in the southern part of the town, known as Cedar Pond. As the time drew near, the news extended far and wide, and extensive preparations were made in every direction to be present on the occasion. Those who had horses, used them; whilst those who had none, travelled on foot, from miles in all directions, to witness the scene. Among others, my father and mother went; but, to my great disappointment, (and it was one of the greatest I had ever experienced,) I was not allowed to witness the baptism.

The hour for the administration of the ordinance arrived, and every available place was said to be occupied. The trees, which were in abundance on the banks, were covered with anxious spectators, and the man of God administered the ancient rite, and those happy souls were buried with Christ in baptism. This baptism was the theme of conversation for weeks in every house and in every place of resort. The mode, its subjects, and its propriety were discussed *pro* and *con;* but, as a general thing, did not meet with favor.

During the administration of the ordinance the hymn was sung which contains the lines—

    "Oh, how happy are they who their Saviour obey,
    And have laid up their treasure above!"

The hymn continued to be sung in almost every place of business for some time. When I first heard it, I became convinced, from all that I had heard of the baptism and its surrounding circumstances, that it must be precisely similar to those as recorded by Matthew.and the other evangelists respecting the baptisms of John and Jesus. And never, from that day until this, have I seen any reason to alter my mind respecting believers' baptism.

After this event, I formed a strong desire to become a Baptist; but this was the last I knew of them for about seven years; never, even, in the meantime listening to any one sermon declaring the particular views of the denomination. From that day I loved them, and thought that if it was the Lord's will, I should be delighted to give myself to the preaching of the word of reconciliation. How often did I feel this when I even despaired of becoming a member of a Baptist church!

CHAPTER III.

I BECOME NEGLIGENT OF RELIGION — ENGAGE MY SER-
VICES TO MR. ELLSWORTH—ALARMING SICKNESS—
ATTENTIONS OF MRS. ELLSWORTH— RECOVERY—MY
FATHER'S SICKNESS AND RECOVERY — I AM AGAIN
ILL—MR. ELLSWORTH'S MISFORTUNE—MY MARRIAGE,
AND LOSS OF CHILD.

I CONTINUED to work for my father, who hired
me out for one dollar per week. Being able to
perform almost as much labor as a man, I was
generally fully occupied during the first three
seasons of the year. At length, being tired of
working for so small a sum, I determined to leave
home and seek occupation with better pay.

I had now arrived at the age of sixteen, and
had become, in great measure, indifferent and
negligent about the concerns of my soul. I began
to look upon the past as a delusion, and concluded
that I had been deceived. My opportunities to
attend the means of grace had been much more
frequent, but I embraced them mostly without
comfort or profit. As I had never mentioned the
subject to any one I now resolved that I would

16

not, lest it should all prove a deception, but determined to live a strictly moral life, thus striving to inculcate the belief that it was all-sufficient unto salvation.

About this time I went to Hartford, where a cousin who resided there had obtained for me a situation with Henry L. Ellsworth, Esq., for ten dollars per month. I commenced for one month on trial, with the mutual agreement, that should he, by the expiration of the term, be dissatisfied with me, he should forward me home. On the other hand, should I be displeased with the place, I should be at liberty to leave at my option.

Mrs. Ellsworth was an enterprising and kind-hearted woman, who desired to see every thing move aright in her presence. It was made my duty to pound the clothes, preparatory to washing, every Sabbath night,—a duty to which I had not been accustomed, and for which I had not yet formed a liking, especially when I had to perform this duty on the evening of the Sabbath. As they kept a carriage, I had also to take care of three horses, and as they almost invariably rode out after the afternoon meetings, I again objected. These things led me to conclude that I should not do more than complete my month with them, as I

was not willing to labor more than six days in the
week, much less on the Sabbath, excepting in cases
of mercy or necessity. I therefore commenced to
make arrangements to leave; to which they objected, showing their unwillingness by offering to
increase my wages. That, however, did not shake
my determination. Madam, at length, pressed me
for my objections. I gave them by telling her
that I believed the holy Sabbath to be a day
appointed for rest, and not for labor, and I could
not, therefore, do what they desired to be performed
on that day. Neither did I desire to interfere with
their arrangements, and considered, therefore, that
it would be much better for us to separate than to
live together in disagreement. Mrs. Ellsworth
then inquired if I should be willing to remain. To
which I replied, that I was willing to work for
any person at any time, excepting on the Sabbath.
As she agreed that it should be discontinued, I
engaged to remain, and did remain for four years,
during which time I found it a home to all intents
and purposes.

In the course of about two years from entering
upon this engagement, I was seized with typhoid
fever, which in the course of a few days assumed
so virulent a form, that my kind friends, and even

physicians, declared that I could not survive.
During all my serious sickness, Mrs. Ellsworth
was unwearied in her attentions to me, both by
night and by day, often watching with me and
administering to my wants for successive nights
with all the solicitude that she could have manifested for her own son. She was often assisted by
her sister-in-law, Mrs. Thomas S. Williams, wife
of the Chief Justice of the State of Connecticut.
Those two ladies, angels of mercy and sisters of
charity, have both long since gone to their rest,
and to receive the reward of Him who has declared that a cup of cold water given to a disciple
should not pass unrewarded. Peace to their
ashes! And sweet to me is the remembrance of
the names of Mrs. Nancy Goodrich Ellsworth and
Mrs. Delia Williams.

About this time I was sent for to return home,
my father being apparently lying at the point of
death. Neither of us knew about the illness of
the other until we were both convalescent. After
the fever turned, which continued about three
weeks, I was made aware of my perilous condition, and felt that, indeed, there had been but a
step between me and death.

For three or four weeks I seemed to recover

most rapidly, when I was suddenly attacked with an affection of the liver, which again brought me almost to the border of the grave, and for two long months I was unable to perform any kind of labor. My pain was so intense, and loss of flesh so rapid, that I could see nothing before me but almost immediate death. My prospects were blighted, and all my earthly hopes and expectations seemed to be destroyed. My ambition was also gone, and my general spirits so low, that I almost decided not to take any more medicine, especially as it was the expressed opinion of my physician that it would be useless.

During this state of my mind and body, the Rev. Dr. Taylor, of New Haven, came to visit Mr. Ellsworth. When he saw me, he pitied me. Being told that I was given up by my physician, he conversed with me very kindly concerning my spiritual condition. Afterwards, before leaving, he recommended to my use " Hadlock's Vegetable Powder." As I had determined to use no more means, I entertained no faith even in doctors' prescriptions. Being apprehensive that I would not procure the medicine, the Doctor himself obtained it, and sent it with kind regards and an earnest request that I would try it. He also sent me special directions for its use. Although with great reluctance, I acceded to his request. I very soon, by God's blessing, became relieved; and before I had taken one and a half bottles, I was nearly freed from pain. Having a good opportunity to go to Saratoga and use the waters freely, I departed almost immediately, and found, in the course of two months' time, that I had so far recovered as to be able to return to my labor. I then returned to my situation, which I had not given up, nor meanwhile had my wages stopped.

About this time Mr. Ellsworth failed, when I left and boarded for a short time. I had for several months been engaged to a lady, and we were now immediately married and commenced housekeeping. Our first child lived to be only nine months old, when the Lord was pleased to take her to Himself. At this time, we were both without the consolations of the gospel, and regarded this as a severe chastisement. Feeling that we had lost our best treasure, and that, in fact, we had lost our all, we determined to break up housekeeping and obtain a situation together, where we could forget our sorrow, and at the same time support ourselves. No long time elapsed before just such an opportunity offered as we had desired.

CHAPTER IV.

THE Hon. Chief Justice Williams, a brother-in-law of the gentleman with whom I had first lived, desired me and my wife to go and live with him, offering me the privilege of working for him or not, according to my choice. We accepted the engagement. My wife soon after became afflicted with physical infirmities of a threatening character, and from which she has never recovered. The result has been, to deprive her of the use of her left knee and right arm.

About this time, the Lord, in His mercy, began again to manifest Himself to my poor soul. I had not been wholly unmindful of His goodness, and was constantly in attendance at the Talcott Street Sabbath-school, of which Mr. Normand Smith was long the Superintendent.* During my attendance at this school, there were several con-

---

* Memoir of Normand Smith.

versions; thinking upon this subject, I began to believe that I must surely be a cast-away, and therefore once more became troubled about my condition. The friends, also, became quite anxious, and reminded me that I had passed through many revivals of religion without giving my heart wholly to God. For a while, I was again deeply anxious, almost realizing that should I suffer present opportunities to pass unheeded, I must at last take up the woeful lamentation of the lost soul, and say, "The harvest is passed, the summer is ended, and I am not saved."

Notwithstanding all this, however, I again became quite careless and indifferent, even to that extent that I absented myself from the Sabbath-school in the morning, which time I spent in sleep. Upon one occasion, I had pursued my now usual practice, yet went to the church in the afternoon, but only to sit down again and go to sleep. Hymns were sung, a prayer was offered, and the Scriptures read, but as yet I was undisturbed. At length the minister arose and announced as his text the words, "Redeeming the time." (Eph. v. 16.) The very reading of these words brought me to my feet, and my feelings were so stirred that I was inclined to leave the house, never again to return.

It seemed to me that I was so much and so continually troubled about the subject of religion, that I had no peace of mind, and thought it would be better for me to forsake all thoughts of it forever. Whilst thus reasoning, however, something appeared to say to me, that were I unmindful and heedless of this admonition, it would be the last. Fully bewildered by this mysterious voice within, I determined to listen attentively to the Word from the mouth of His servant. I then heard a sermon—the first for a long time—and I trust a profitable one, which I hope never to forget.

This occurred in the Talcott Street Meeting-house, which, although originated and completed chiefly through the influence and by the money of the Baptists, at the time referred to was a "union church." It was one of the places where members of all denominations sometimes worshipped, sometimes quarrelled. When there was nothing else to contend about, the Baptists were accused of believing that they were better than other Christians, and none but themselves would ever reach heaven. Being tired of these unprofitable harangues, and also a believer in the Baptist doctrine, especially in the ordinance of baptism, and believed that immersion, and immersion of believers

only, was Scriptural baptism, I left, and attended
the First Baptist Church. Talcott Street Meeting-
house afterwards went into the possession of the
Presbyterians.

After some time spent in deliberation and
prayer, I was baptized in the river by the Rev.
Gustavus F. Davis, D. D., and united with the
First Baptist Church. Then all things seemed well.
I was deeply interested in all the public exercises—more particularly, perhaps, in the Prayer
and Conference Meetings, from which I derived
great benefit, and in which I was frequently
invited by the pastor to take a part.

Owing to the state of my wife's health, I found
it necessary to take board for her. In a short
time after, she presented me with a fine son,
who lived to be five months of age, and was so
early taken away from us. He died suddenly,
and I arrived only in time for him to die in my
arms. Great as the loss appeared to be at this
time, I felt perfectly resigned to the will of God,
and could with Christian resignation say, "The
Lord gave, and the Lord hath taken away; blessed
be the name of the Lord!" For the first time, I
felt what it was to be sustained in the day of trial,
and comforted by the grace of God.

2 B

After having united with the church, I felt a strong desire to be useful to my fellow-men in some way, and was deeply impressed with a desire to preach the Gospel; but reflecting upon my ignorance, the few opportunities of improvement within my reach, and my ideas touching the general duties of a preacher of Christ, I endeavored to banish the idea from my mind, without mentioning it to any one.

Since, however, my mind has undergone a very considerable change respecting the requisite qualifications for the Gospel ministry. I may, perhaps, as well state them here as elsewhere:

My views of "a call to the Gospel ministry," so far, at least, as my knowledge is concerned, may be very simply stated:

First: I believe that the candidate must be wholly regenerated by the Holy Spirit.

Second: That he must be called of God, and possessed of an irrepressible desire for the work, not for any pecuniary or social advantage which may accrue, but for the work's sake, that souls may be converted, the church edified, and the Lord Jesus glorified.

Third: That he must be willing to perform any act of self-denial in order to accomplish it, feeling that a present and eternal woe rests upon him if he preaches not the Gospel.

Fourth: That he make himself acquainted with the Word of God. It is this that he must study to prove himself to be a workman that needeth not to be ashamed, that when going forth and bearing precious seed he may return rejoicing.

Fifth: That he should possess an unquenchable love for the souls of sinners, that he may be willing to do all things and bear all things, looking for his reward in the promise that "they that turn many to righteousness shall shine as the stars in the firmament for ever and ever."

I cannot but feel that he who entertains such views and is exercised by such feelings as described above is called of God as was Aaron.

Having thus briefly given my views of what I consider to be the main points involved in a call to the ministry, I will now narrate the principal facts touching my entrance upon the sacred calling.

On consultation with my beloved pastor, he advised me to be constant in my attendance on the means of grace, and exercise my gift on every fitting opportunity. Being, however, naturally diffident, and knowing that there were but three colored male members of a church whose whole

membership was about four hundred, including
nearly forty colored sisters, I generally refrained
from taking any part in the public exercises unless
called upon, notwithstanding that I knew myself
to be the recipient of their Christian affection and
regard, and would most willingly have been heard
by them. Their fraternal feelings were manifested
in many ways; among others, by always appoint-
ing me on committees of discipline, and generally
as chairman when any difficulty occurred with
any of my own color.

I was at this time residing with the Hon. T. S.
Williams, as his servant. Upon one pleasant
morning, when proceeding to my day's labor, I
was very unexpectedly thrown into the company
of Deacon Jeremiah Brown, one of the deacons of
the church, who, in the course of conversation,
greatly to my surprise, conversed with me respecting my duty to preach the Gospel, stating,
also, that such was the opinion of the brethren
generally. Seeing obstacles in the way, I could
not but name them. I reminded him of my lack
of education, without which I thought no minister was fit to teach. I next advanced as an
objection the fact that my wife was an invalid,
and therefore entirely dependent upon me for

support, quoting at the same time the Scripture which saith that "he who provideth not for his own house has denied the faith, and is worse than an infidel."

I stated my views fully and freely, maintaining that under such circumstances that however much I might desire the work of the ministry, I could not enter upon it until these formidable obstacles were removed, when I would give myself wholly to the Lord, forgetting that I had already professed to do so, when I had reason to believe that He by His grace had made me a new creature in Christ Jesus.

The good deacon remarked, in return, that he considered that the requisite qualifications to preach Christ and Him crucified did not wholly depend upon the amount of scholastic knowledge the individual might possess, desirable though it was. The main point in his judgment was that there should be realized a special call from God, which, he insisted upon, would be a surety of success. After stating that he would mention the interview to the brethren of the church, that he might ascertain their views and purposes more definitely, he inquired as to the length of time and amount of expense which I supposed to be required to prepare me for the work. My reply was, that perhaps two years and three hundred dollars might, under all the circumstances, be sufficient. Then, after promising him that if the means could be obtained I would sincerely devote myself to the work, we parted.

Not long after this interview, I was favored with a call from a gentleman who came to make me a proposition to go into the country and take charge of a farm—an offer which I immediately declined on the ground of the ill health of my wife, which I considered to incapacitate her from superintending that department which would require her special attention. My visitor, however, prevailed upon me to withhold a final decision and consider the matter more fully, on the plea that my wife's health, whilst her labor would not be required, would be greatly improved, and that my own pecuniary advantage would be materially advanced. We thereupon parted, leaving the matter unsettled for a few days.

Upon consultation with my wife, I was happily surprised to find her not only willing, but even anxious, that I should accept the proffered engagement, partly because of her confidence in the gentleman who had made the proposal, as he was

a surgeon. I could not but regard her willingness as the result of the interposition of Providence, the more especially as I had concealed
from my wife the main reason which had influenced me in accepting the proposition.

But a few days elapsed, and the gentleman
again called upon me, according to appointment,
when I made a written agreement with him on
advantageous terms for one year, believing that
at its expiration I should be enabled to commence
my studies. Arrangements being made, our
removal was soon effected.

My wife's health now very much improved,
although she never recovered wholly the use of
her limbs. About three months after our entrance
upon our new and pleasant home, my employer,
desiring to make some alterations on his premises
that he might extend his operations, proposed, as
his wish, that I should extend my term of service
from one to five years. To this I objected. He
then became dissatisfied and expressed a desire
that the agreement should be cancelled, desiring
me to name the conditions upon which I would
give up the bargain. So, I then made a proposal
with a view to my preparation for the ministry.
He accepted my proposition, upon condition that I

was to continue until the crops were gathered. Thus the Lord enabled me, in less than one year, to obtain all the funds necessary for my education and to support my family.

The Lord had been very good to me. He had heard my prayer and granted my request. Here I can see an illustration of that Scripture which says, "In the Lord's hands are the hearts of all men, and He can turn them as the rivers of water are turned."

CHAPTER V.

OFTEN do I blame myself, and shall do unto
my dying day, that I did not receive a good education. At the time of which I am about to
speak, I fell into a sore temptation. It presented
itself to me in this form. I believed that it was
by my business tact and skill, that I had been
enabled to accomplish what is related in the last
chapter. It was very easy, therefore, for me not
only to forget my promise to my Saviour, and the
mysterious way in which He had led me, but, also,
my conversation with my brother, the deacon.
When I reflect upon it, I cannot but think it now
as impossible—certainly, not less than strange.

I then began to reason in this way: I commenced with nothing, and now I have something
wherewith to start. I have been blessed beyond
my most sanguine expectations. Surely, by close
attention to business, I cannot fail to succeed. I

2 *   33

was then so elated with the mere idea of making money, that it seemed like the opening of a new era in the history of my life.

I immediately made arrangements to go into business with a manufacturing concern. My duty was to carry their wares into the city, and bring back, in return, coal and steel, at a given price per cwt., thus insuring employment for every day in the year. I furnished two of the finest teams in town and commenced my work; and when I invested my capital, I could not see, nor can I now see, the possibility of my failing, unless I was under God's disapprobation.

Alas! alas! what is man when left to himself! "He may appoint, but God disappoints." For six months, every thing went wrong with me, until I found myself, pecuniarily, much in about the same condition at the expiration of that time as at the beginning. Yet in my blindness and ignorance, I could not understand it. I was so blind, as well as ignorant, that I did not see that I had provoked the Lord to anger, and that He had, therefore, forsaken me. I still attended to my religious duties, both privately and publicly, but I did not find happiness and comfort in them as formerly, nor did I receive much benefit.

For two years, I did not discover the cause of my disappointment. About this time, I returned to the city. I found that during my absence, my pastor had deceased, and that Rev. Henry Jackson was his successor, whom I highly esteemed; but, having little acquaintance with him, I could not approach him with that degree of confidence that I could the pastor who baptized me. He continued with the church only about one year after my return; but owing to the peculiar state of my mind, I did not form so strong an attachment to him as I should have done, or as he was worthy of receiving from me.

The year passed, during which I continued my attendance upon the means of grace, for I still loved the assembly of God's people and the place where His honor dwelleth. Yet I was driven almost to despair. That year I shall never forget.

During the same year, my wife presented me with another daughter, thus adding to my little household one to supply the place of the dear children we had buried with so much grief.

Some time after my return to the city, a singular and novel circumstance occurred. There were situated at that time, in the gallery of the meeting-house, two large pews, capable of holding some twenty persons. The pews, situated at the corner of the galleries, were separated from the other seats by partitions, about three feet high, between the minister and his colored hearers, which concealed them mainly from the view of the congregation and minister. They contained but two or three choice seats, one of which it was my privilege frequently to occupy. Having lost this, upon a certain afternoon, the only available seat in the pew was one which would place my back to the preacher, and my head but a little higher than the top of the pew. I could not but feel indignant at the idea of sitting thus, when there was an abundance of unoccupied seats in other parts of the galleries. This one subject engrossed my mind during the services, and I determined never to sit in that seat again—not even to prevent my exclusion from the church. I was grieved to leave the temple, remembering my baptism and covenant, the many delightful prayer-meetings which I had attended, and instructive sermons to which I had listened. It was to me a solemn step to take, but there seemed to be a principle involved which I had no right to surrender.

I then returned to the Union Church in Talcott Street, where the Lord had been pleased in a

great degree to bless my poor soul. I was received
with much kindness and reminded of certain pre-
dictions that had been uttered, which some of
the brethren thought were now verily fulfilled. I
resolved that hereafter I would worship with the
brethren of this place.

Inquiries being made after me, from time to
time, by the brethren of the First Church, it was
not long ere I was visited by the deacons to ascertain the cause of my protracted absence. We
conversed with perfect freedom. I maintained my
my own cause to the best of my ability, assuring
them, in addition, that I left mainly to avoid a
collision with the church. They tried to convince
me of what they deemed to be an error, but all to
no purpose.

The deacons reported the whole matter to the
church, when a very spirited discussion ensued,
which resulted in a vote that the colored members
should occupy the vacant seats in the gallery at
their pleasure.

A committee, appointed to state to me the action
of the church, informed me that the pews erected
for colored persons were condemned, as causing
distinction and dissatisfaction among the members
of the body of Christ, and furthermore that it

was their intention to propose the construction of other pews in their stead. I replied that I was pleased with their action, and in their proposal to remove those (to me) objectionable seats. But why reconstruct them, whilst so many vacant pews remain in the church, unless you wish to colonize the colored people?

Notwithstanding the many and strong objections urged, the new seats were erected. They were similar to all others in the gallery, excepting in size. Notice was given that on a certain day they would be let to the colored members, who were respectfully invited to be present.

The time of sale came, yet but one colored woman was present, who, having chosen her pew, expressed her belief that I was the cause of the absence of the colored members.

Another day was fixed, but with little better success. I was, indeed, considered to be the obstacle in the way of their rental. The pews having cost about one hundred dollars, very much anxiety was expressed by many that the church should be indemnified. Furthermore, if rented at all, they must be rented to colored people.

This new phase of the question, with the whole trouble, soon again occupied the attention of the church, when it was deemed expedient to appoint a committee, to consist of the pastor, Rev. Henry Jackson, Rev. Gurdon Robins, and deacons Joseph B. Gilbert, Jeremiah Brown, and Aaron Clapp. The committee were appointed to meet the colored members of the church at one of the sister's houses.

The parties being present on the day and hour of appointment, the pastor called upon me to open the meeting with prayer. He afterwards stated the object which had brought us together, the great interest which he felt in the colored portion of his church, and expressed his anxiety that the whole matter should soon be brought to an amicable conclusion. The pastor then commenced questioning the members respecting their objections to the seats which had been provided for them by the church, and why they had not complied with the wish of the church. Most of them answered that they had no objection, but, on the other hand, were much pleased with them. Some of them even expressed their intention to rent them.

No one, but God alone, knows, or ever will know, the feelings of my heart that day. I was disappointed in my brethren and sisters. They had made numerous complaints to me, and de-

clared their intention to stand by me to the last.
"O!" I thought, "is this your kindness to your
friend?" Then I saw what oppression had done
to break the spirits of the colored people, and how
soon they yield to, rather than contend against,
those whom they regard as their superiors.

"Well," I thought, "I am in bad company, and
surely I must pay dearly for it. But, neverthe-
theless, the cause is a righteous one." I was
strengthened as I never was before. It came my
turn to speak for myself, and I truly felt happy
that it was so. Not that I expected to accomplish
any thing more than to unburden my feelings, for
I was pressed like a cart beneath a heavy load.
It was the first time that I had ever been called
upon to stand up in the defence of the rights of
my brethren. I endeavored to show that we were
not the aggressors in this movement. We had
only asked what the church was willing volunta-
rily to grant; and, what was more, all that we
needed; the other was gratuitous and uncalled
for; and for them to draw a line of demarcation
between white and colored members of the same
family, and then ask us to pay for this colonization
in the house of God, seemed to me to be unreason-
able and unchristian. We would have been will-

ing, without any expense, to have paid for our sittings in the gallery; and, if they had not been disposed to give both sides, we would have taken one side, which we could nearly fill. But for one, I was not prepared to have any thing to do with this arrangement, and solemnly declined paying even one cent. If my brethren and sisters would take my advice, they would never enter into such an agreement, for I believed the scheme originated in the prejudice of one portion of the church against the other, and I should sin against God if I were to give it my sanction. My address on this subject was continued about half an hour, and I sat down relieved and refreshed. No one attempted to reply, but a resolution was offered by one of the committee to drop the whole subject, and allow the colored persons to sit where they pleased in the galleries. This was agreed to by the committee, and, at a subsequent meeting of the church, adopted, and thus ended this painful and unpleasant difficulty, and peace and harmony were restored.

It is proper I should say, in closing the account of the above incident, that my objection to sitting in the colored pew arose not more from an instinctive sense of the degradation thus unjustly put

B 2

upon me by the church, than from a religious conviction that I ought to bear my testimony against such wrong towards my race. The second chapter of St. James had clearly taught me that such distinction in the house of God was contrary to the spirit of Christianity. I knew that an evil which Scripture rebuked, I might myself protest against.

I was still in a state of comparative darkness, and seemed to enjoy but little of God's presence. About this time, a strong desire manifested itself on the part of the colored brethren and sisters to worship elsewhere, as a separate organization, such being considered as expedient for their best interests, notwithstanding all the kindness which they had received from the members of the First Church.

CHAPTER VI.

RESIGNATION OF REV. HENRY JACKSON—COMMENCEMENT
OF SEPARATE MEETINGS—OUR EMBARRASSMENT UN-
DER THE LOSS OF A PREACHER—ORDINATION OF REV.
J. S. EATON.

ABOUT this time, our pastor resigned his charge
of the church. This seemed to help forward the
desire of the colored brethren and sisters to have
the separate meeting. The matter was talked over
with some of the members of the church, and it
was thought desirable to establish a colored Baptist church in the city. It was also believed that
many of the colored people would attend, who
could not be induced to go to the white church.
This view of the subject gained favor with the brethren, who agreed that we might make the attempt
upon the following conditions: 1st. That we could
secure the labors of some one to preach for us for
a reasonable compensation; and 2d. That we were
to attend the communion regularly. About this
time, there was a good brother in the Second
Baptist Church who had just been licensed at

43

a place. His services were secured, and we commenced our meetings in a school-house, in Cooper Lane, known as Bliss's tan-yard. We were much pleased with the brother. He was poor, and worked at his trade, as carpenter. We agreed to give him two dollars per Sabbath. He continued with us about one month, when he received a call to settle with a church in Tariffville, which he accepted, and removed forthwith. We were now left without one to break unto us the bread of life. After this, the Rev. Gurdon Robins, an ordained minister in our church, who was accustomed to supply destitute churches in the country, hire a conveyance which cost him two dollars and a half per week, ride over the mountains some ten or twelve miles, through the inclemency of the winter, and get for his service five dollars a Sabbath, seeing that we were destitute, he agreed to supply us during the winter for two dollars a Sabbath. This seemed quite providential. We made an agreement with him to supply us for the winter. He commenced his labors with us, and we thanked God, and took courage, and went on. He continued some four Sabbaths. During this time, we changed our location, and hired a room on the main street, a few doors above the Central Presbyterian Church.

Soon after our removal, one Sabbath afternoon, brother Robins requested me to remain, after preaching, as he had something he wished to communicate to me. Much to my surprise, he told me he did not think he could preach for us any longer. I inquired the reason for this unexpected and sudden change in his views. He replied that he could not tell, but it did seem to him not to be his duty to remain. I asked him if he did not receive his pay according to agreement. He answered, so far as that was concerned, he was perfectly satisfied, but he felt, notwithstanding, he could not continue, and yet he could not give the reason. He wished me to inform the brethren that he could not serve them any longer. This I declined, telling him that he must come the next Sabbath, and tell his own story, to which he finally agreed. There were three colored brethren, besides myself, Primous Babcock, Zadi Jones, and Henry Jackson. During the week, I communicated to them the intelligence which I had received, and they were astonished and confounded. We all felt cast down, and almost discouraged, but said nothing about it to the sisters, hoping that the brother might be prevailed on to change his mind. We saw him, and said all to him that we could. We thought our prospects were flattering. We spoke of our fears that the interest would go down, and prove a failure, but all to no purpose. He said he must not do it; but he entertained no fears of our ultimate success. He believed the Lord had a hand in it, but could not at present understand His design, yet advised us to continue in prayer, and wait on the Lord, and we should see his salvation.

The next Sabbath came; the brother preached his farewell sermon, and commended us to the care of our heavenly Father. It was a weeping time. We felt that all of these things were against us. But we resolved to go on, and trust in the Lord. It again fell to my lot to obtain supplies, in which duty I had been very successful. We were seldom without some one to break to us the bread of life. During the balance of the winter, we held regular prayer and conference meetings, and they were comforting and refreshing, and thus the Lord provided for us, and brought us to behold the spring.

About this time, Rev. John Lewis, a free-will

Baptist, visited Hartford, and preached for us a few times. We were pleased with him, and invited him to supply us for a time. He signified his willingness to labor with us for six months, if we desired it, if we could raise him twenty-five dollars per month. We doubted our ability to meet this sum; but after deliberation upon the matter, we agreed to lay it before the church, and ask their advice, which we did. They finally concluded, if we were desirous to retain him, we might do so; but we must continue our connection with the first church as formerly; and what we lacked of making up his salary, they would assist us to raise.

He commenced his labors with us. Our hopes were buoyant, and our prospects were more flattering than ever. Our congregations increased, so that our place, which would accommodate about one hundred and fifty or two hundred, was quite full every Sabbath afternoon.

Mr. Lewis continued to preach for us with great acceptance about one month. He then asked leave of absence for two weeks to visit his family, and bring his wife to Hartford, and spend the summer. This was unanimously agreed to. We had no trouble about raising his money, and he left with the understanding that he would return in two or three weeks at the farthest. I was again appointed to obtain a supply. I worked hard during the day, and in the evenings would look for some one to break unto us the bread of eternal life. One month rolled on, and we heard nothing from our brother. Another month passed away, and yet we had no tidings from him. The people were much discouraged and perplexed. Very much to our surprise, four or five months elapsed before we even heard *of* his whereabouts, but never were able to ascertain the reason of his peculiar course, which had so much embarrassed us. It was still my duty to procure supplies, and I am not aware that I ever took more delight than in soliciting brethren to preach the Word.

It had now got to be autumn, and the winter was drawing nigh. We seemed to have no hope of procuring any one, and it became quite a serious consideration with some of us whether we had not better disband, and return to the church which we were all confident would welcome us home. I went so far as to propose to the members the propriety of this course, and very strenuously to advocate it. I found I was the only one that had any desire for it. They said they would sooner meet together, and sing and pray, than to think of such a course. They were determined to wait on the Lord, and see what he had in store for them.

They charged me with being faithless. One good old sister, a thorough-going Baptist, a firm believer in the doctrine of sovereign grace, who has oftentimes strengthened and encouraged me, said to me, "My dear brother, God will provide. Do not get weary in well doing, for in due season we shall reap, if we faint not."

We resolved, therefore, to go on until we should see what the Lord would do for us. We really felt that there was a blessing in store even for us. I agreed to continue to procure supplies when ever it was possible.

Meanwhile, the "mother" church called another pastor, brother J. S. Eaton, from Maine, who was subsequently ordained; Rev. Dr. Stow, of Boston, preaching a most impressive and eloquent discourse from the words, "He was an eloquent man, and mighty in the Scriptures." (Acts xviii. 24.)

The impression that sermon made on my mind I shall never forget. I saw in it more relating to

3 c

the work of the ministry than I had ever seen before. I was led to ask, "Lord, who is sufficient for these things?" But he anticipated my inquiry, and showed that his sufficiency was of the Lord. The church was once more blessed with a pastor, who commanded the esteem and affection of his people.

CHAPTER VII.

THE time had now arrived when the Lord was
again pleased to manifest himself to my poor soul,
for which I desire to praise his holy name through
time and eternity. It seemed as though he would
not let me go, although I had so richly merited
his divine displeasure. After a while, I began to
find it exceedingly difficult to obtain supplies for
our new interest. On one cold and stormy Saturday, I sought diligently for some one to preach to
us on the morrow, devoting, I think, the most of
the day to that purpose. But I sought in vain.
Disappointed, perplexed, and weary, I returned
to my home. The evening was to me one fraught
with intense anxiety. Even domestic comforts
and the prattling of my little daughter failed to
lift the shadow from my mind. Thus discouraged,
I retired to rest, in the vain hope of losing myself
for a while in forgetfulness. But even in sleep,

51

which came tardily upon me, the question, who
will preach on the coming Sabbath, occupied my
thoughts. Awaking suddenly from my feverish
sleep, I imagined that I heard a voice, speaking
in tones as loud as thunder, "Preach yourself!"
I immediately arose and fell upon my knees before
the Lord, when it seemed to me as if all my experience and all the circumstances of the past three
years flashed with the speed and vividness of
lightning upon my mind, from the conversation
which I first had with deacon Brown until the
present time. My emotions were so overpowering
for a few moments, that I fancied myself to be
utterly undone. A sense of the goodness of God
arose before me with stupendous magnitude. I
felt that He had especially favored me, granting
all my requests; yea, He had even given me more
than I had asked. When I reflected upon this,
in contrast with my own loose conduct, I felt
ashamed and condemned, realizing my unfaithful-
ness, and that my time and means for preparation
were gone. I was convinced the Lord required
me immediately to comply with the command of
the Saviour and the promises which I had made,
but still my heart rebelled; I was unwilling to
preach Christ to expose my ignorance, believing

it to be a most severe ordeal for any man, not thoroughly educated, to expose himself to the criticisms of those who might be better informed. I remained on my knees until self was conquered and my soul was blessed. I now consider this almost as great a work as was first wrought in my soul at its conversion. A perfect resignation possessed me, and I promised the Lord, that night, that I would go just as I was and work in His vineyard in any portion or capacity He might see fit to appoint. I had done with dictation, and felt that I had nothing then to do but to obey. The language of my heart was, "Lord, what wilt thou have me do?" I promised that I would commence on the very next day, if He so directed, and, furthermore, formed a resolution that, should I live until the coming Sabbath, I would communicate to my brethren what the Lord had done for me, and how, at last, he had conquered me.

The hour of the Sabbath morning, for which I had been very impatient, at length arrived when I should meet with my brethren and sisters, and relate to them the Lord's special dealings with me during the past two or three years. Having arrived at the place of meeting, after introductory services, I arose and informed them of my failure to procure a supply, how the Lord had made Himself known to me in this matter, and what, by His gracious help, I intended to attempt. Then followed a weeping time. We wept and rejoiced together. The brethren thanked God for what He had done, and prayed that He would give me strength to keep my vows. They then invited me to speak for them in the afternoon of the same day, an invitation which I accepted most thankfully, throwing myself entirely into the Lord's hands, believing that He would sustain me. I found, in the afternoon, that a larger congregation than usual was gathered, many being probably drawn there by motives of curiosity. I used as my text the fourth verse of the second chapter of Jonah, being, as I thought, most appropriate to the existing circumstances. "Then I said, I am cast out of Thy sight; yet will I look again toward Thy holy temple." The brethren professed to be edified and instructed, and bidding me "God-speed!" insisted upon my continuing to speak to them, which I did every Sabbath afternoon until the following Spring.

Very soon after I commenced to preach, two or three of the brethren of the parent church called upon me with the request that I would speak before them on some Wednesday evening, which, after some hesitation, I consented to do. When the evening came, as it had been circulated that I was to preach in the First Baptist Meeting-house, we had a much larger gathering of the church and congregation than usual. When I arrived at the lecture-room and saw what a concourse of people had gathered, I was completely overpowered. I got just inside the door, and sat down in a chair, and I think I could never have gone to the pulpit if my pastor had not come and taken me by the hand, and led me to the desk. I endeavored to address them from these words: "Seek ye first the kingdom of God and His righteousness, and all these things shall be added unto you." (Matt. vi. 33.)

After I had concluded, the pastor made some remarks expressive of his appreciation of the discourse, being followed by one of the deacons, who also avowed his entire approbation. The Rev. Gurdon Robins then remarked, that since he had heard my defence before the committee appointed by the church to investigate certain difficulties with the colored members, he had been convinced that I was called to preach the Gospel. A motion was then made by one of the deacons, and unanimously adopted, to the effect, "That brother Jeremiah Asher receive the approbation of this church to preach the Gospel whenever and wherever opportunity is presented."

The following is a copy of the formal license:—

"This may certify that the bearer, Jeremiah Asher, is a member in full standing and fellowship with us, and we believe that he has gifts, which, if improved, will render him useful in the ministry. We therefore cordially recommend him to improve his talents whenever God, in His providence, shall open a door.

"Done by order and in behalf of the First Baptist Church, Hartford, Connecticut. March, 1839."

J. B. GILBERT,   } *Deacons.*
JEREMIAH BROWN, }
JOSEPH W. DIMOCK, *Ch. Clk.*
J. S. EATON, *Pastor.*

CHAPTER VIII.

AFTER having obtained the approbation of the
church, my mind became much exercised about
leaving Hartford to go elsewhere, in order to
improve myself in general knowledge. I realized
that I had squandered many precious opportunities, and that it now became me to "redeem the
time." After much meditation and prayer, I
determined on going to Providence, R. I. I then
communicated my decision to my colored brethren and sisters, telling them that, as dearly as I
loved them, I felt it to be my duty to leave them,
at the same time giving them the reasons which
had brought me to this conclusion. Although
with great reluctance, they at length expressed
agreement with my opinion as to the desirable-
ness of the movement.

3 * 57

At a subsequent conference meeting of the church, when, however, but few were present on account of the inclemency of the weather, I brought the whole matter before them, and requested assistance for myself, and that they would pay some attention to my helpless family, during my absence, which I did not at that time suppose would be protracted beyond four or five weeks. They cheerfully complied with my request, and some few of the brethren subscribed a sufficient amount to pay my travelling expenses; but, after dividing with my wife, I found that I had but five dollars remaining.

A few days afterwards, notwithstanding the reluctance of my wife, who could not see it to be my duty to take the step which I had proposed, and leave my family in a helpless condition— having made my arrangements, I started on my journey of seventy miles, on a cold spring day, with but one dollar in my purse, after having paid my fare. The thought of this caused me to waver. I was going, without means, to a place where I knew not a single individual, but yet my trust was in God.

I was alone in the stage-coach for the greater part of the journey, being the only "through" passenger. Then, I could not but think that, if there is such a thing as Satan being permitted to make a direct personal attack, he was making a severe onslaught upon me by placing before me a severe temptation ; for, had the stage stopped at some convenient place, I was inclined to alight and return to my home. Many embarrassing thoughts passed through my mind. I reflected that I was going among a strange people, who, for aught I knew, were neither liberal nor hospitable. I was without money. From what source, then, could I expect subsistence. It might be, that among all the colored population, there were no Baptists. Besides, I had no acquaintances whatever in the city. Nevertheless, natural and discouraging as these thoughts were, casting me down almost to the lowermost depths of fear, I determined to proceed, and in due time was landed at the Manufacturers' Hotel, where I engaged board for three dollars per week, trusting to the interposing help of Divine Providence.

Having taken with me a letter of introduction from my pastor to one of his old classmates, the late Rev. M. M. Dean, then pastor of the Third Baptist Church in Providence, after a night's rest, I hastened to deliver it. Not finding him home,

I lengthened my walk. On returning to the hotel, I found that he had called and left an invitation for me to renew my attempt to see him, and partake of his hospitality by dining with him. On the following day, I enjoyed a very pleasant interview, and, although no reference was made to the object of my visit, I felt much cheered and encouraged. When about to leave, Mr. Dean informed me that a sister of my late pastor desired to see me. Although she was at the time very sick, and refused to receive most of her visitors, yet she desired to have an interview with me.

At the hour appointed on the following day, I found access to the sick chamber, and received from Miss Phebe Jackson a hearty welcome. At her own request, I gave her fully the reasons for my visiting Providence, communicating to her my desires, and the action of the First Church in Hartford. After expressing her opinion that the church should have provided the means, she suggested that some way might be opened by which I could extend my knowledge of geography, arithmetic, and grammar, manifested very much interest in my project, and encouraged me to persevere. She desired me to call again on the following day, hoping, in the meantime, to procure

me lodgings where my expenses would be reduced. On my retiring, she placed in my hands
five dollars, and bade me God-speed. I was compelled to regard this as an interposition of Divine
Providence, for no one in the city could be acquainted with the slenderness of my pecuniary
means. I was well clad, and had not, and
did not intend to mention to any one my pecuniary necessities, thinking, if the Lord had sent
me, He would provide. I therefore praised the
Lord for His goodness in providing for me that
which I most lacked at this peculiar juncture.

On the following day, according to appointment, I again called upon Miss Jackson, and
found, to my delight, that she had procured for
me a temporary home with a family formerly of
Hartford, who appeared to be acquainted with
me. There I remained for two months, meanwhile
receiving instruction daily from two of the students of Brown University. I afterwards received
much valuable instruction from the Rev. Dr. Dow-
ling, who was at that time pastor of one of the
Baptist churches in Providence. To him my
thanks are always due. Gratified by my progress,
those gentlemen suggested the expediency of my
being sent to Newton Theological Seminary.

Acting upon this, Miss Jackson procured the aid of the Rev. Mr. Dean to correspond with the President of that institution. The reply was most favorable, and he consented to take me for two years. I verily thought then that the way was clear, and my prospects brighter than ever. But how mysterious are the designs of God, and His ways past finding out!

About the same time, another object was presented to my consideration. A church edifice, used for some years as a "Union" Meeting-house, but owned principally by the colored members of the regular Baptist churches of the city—recently occupied by the Free-will Baptists—now becoming available, it was suggested to form a new Baptist interest, that I should abandon all idea of going to Newton, and accept its charge. A number of the members of the First Church were particularly desirous that this plan should succeed. The project was presented to me in such a manner, that, reluctant as I was to abandon my anticipated course of study, I felt that my duty was clear, especially as the propositions came from so respectable a source. Miss Jackson, however, considering it best to leave the whole matter with the church, for its decision, I was willing that my future should be so determined. Having now decided to visit my family, this "mother in Israel," in connection with other Christian ladies, who had shown me many other kindnesses, most generously paid all my expenses of board and education for the two months that had passed. Herein I could see what the Lord is willing to do for those who trust Him. Surely he is round about those who fear and love His holy name.

Previous to my leaving for home, some prominent members of the First Baptist Church in Providence wrote to the First Baptist Church in Hartford, laying before them all the facts in the case. My own church agreed with that in Providence; they advised me to give up the project of going to Newton, and content myself with such opportunities for obtaining instruction as might be afforded in Providence. My brethren gave the following as their reasons for this recommendation: 1st. As I was getting somewhat advanced in life, I should be admonished that whatsoever I expected to do for Christ, I should do quickly; and 2d. That the whole arrangement in relation to the proposed organization of the new interest seemed to be the result of my labors. My duty was, therefore, in their opinion, plainly indicated by the

leadings of Providence. Upon this, I yielded
my judgment to what I considered the better
judgment of the churches, and have ever believed
that I was directed by the Lord.

Although the incident does not chronologically
follow, I will close this chapter by a relation of
one of the most humorous events of my life,
giving some account of one of my trips from Providence to New York. I believe that it occurred
very soon after my settlement in the former city.
I had embarked in one of the steamers plying
between the two cities, on my way to attend a
convention to be held in Philadelphia. Although
I paid the full cabin fare, the captain refused to
give me a ticket for a berth, but assured me, in
the presence of the steward, that he would give
him directions, at the proper time, to provide me
with one. The steamboat train from Boston
brought an unusually large number of passengers,
and as all of the berths would be required, I
saw there was no hope for me. We were soon
under way for New York. The captain sent for
me to make my appearance at his office. Declining to go, he repeated the summons, when,
with my curiosity a little aroused, I presented
myself before the window of the office. He desired

to see my ticket, which he took from my hands, giving me, in return, another, a deck ticket, with fifty cents, at the same time very suddenly closing his window. (This being an opposition boat, the cabin fare was one dollar, and the deck fare fifty cents.) For a moment I was amazed, but, upon consideration, very soon saw the drift of the trick. I concluded that I would try and be even with him. Therefore, although it was yet quite early in the evening, I sought the steward, of whom I requested a berth, that I might retire. He recommended me to wait until after supper, which I would gladly have done under other circumstances. But I strenuously urged my desire for rest. After very much parleying, he at length granted my request, and showed me my berth, when, contrary to my habit when travelling, I undressed and retired. I intended not to be removed very easily. About eleven o'clock, as the captain and clerk were taking their rounds to examine tickets, they came to me. I was apparently in a sound slumber, but, shaking me most violently, they almost drew me from my berth. I rolled back, and apparently slept on, when the captain said to the clerk, "You must wake him, for he has only a deck ticket." Then

c 2

they undertook to search me, but I still *slept.* Giving it up as hopeless, after another ineffectual shaking, the captain said, "Well, let him alone. But in all my life I never saw a man sleep so heavily."

I would mention, as a pleasing sequel to the foregoing, a fact in connection with my few hours' stay in New York. Upon my arrival, I received an invitation to preach in the Zion Baptist Church in the evening, and to supply their pulpit on the following Sabbath. I hesitated how to decide, being anxious to move on immediately to Philadelphia. But yet I had not the means to pay my passage. I did not intend to ask for assistance. This I have never done for that special purpose. When the time of the evening appointment came, I went and preached from a part of the nineteenth verse of the fourteenth chapter of Paul's Epistle to the Roman's, "Let us therefore follow after the things which make for peace." When I had concluded, a lady, whom I had never before met, placed a bill in my hand, saying that the sermon to which she had just listened was to her at least worth that much. Upon examination, I found that she had presented me with three dollars, just my passage money to Philadelphia. I therefore decided to proceed onwards immediately, and spend a Sabbath with my friends of the Zion Church on my return. On my arrival in Philadelphia, I met with the Rev. Daniel Scott, pastor of the Union Baptist Church, preached for him on the Sabbath, and continued to labor with his people for four or five weeks. This was the commencement of my work for Christ in Philadelphia, little supposing that that city was to be the field of so many years of future labor.

CHAPTER IX.

I HAVE, indeed, learned by experience that

"God moves in a mysterious way
His wonders to perform."

His dealings with me have been always merciful and gracious. Yet many a time, when He has led me in a new path, although I could feel His hand, I could not understand the way. Had I not walked by the faith which He imparted, I should have multiplied my crooked paths.

After spending about one month with my family and friends, believing now, as led by the counsel of the churches, that I had an important work to do, I returned to Providence, whence I was soon permitted to send for my family. My first duty was to make arrangements for the organization of the church. This done, a council convened on the ninth day of December, 1840.

The council was composed of delegates from the First, Second, Third, and Fourth churches of Providence; First Church, Pawtucket; and the Independent Church of Boston. The church was organized in due form with the unanimous approbation of the council. It was originally composed of seven brethren and two sisters, one of whom was a confirmed invalid, and very seldom able to attend upon the public means of grace. The public service of recognition took place in the afternoon.

On the evening of that day, having been previously examined by the same council, I was ordained to the work of the Gospel ministry, the Rev. George Black preaching the ordination ser-sermon from 2 Timothy iv. 2—"Preach the Word."

The first Sabbath, January, 1841, we had a candidate for baptism, an elderly lady, about seventy years of age, by the name of Olive Seepet. The day was bitter cold. Our place to administer the ordinance was in the Narragansett River, quite the southern boundary of the city. As I went down into the water with this candidate, I felt quite nervous; but I thought I must say a word by way of comfort to my subject, so I commenced by saying to her, "Don't be afraid."

She replied, "It is you that is afraid, not me." I then proceeded to baptize her in the name of the Father, Son, and Holy Ghost.

A circumstance transpired about this time to which my memory often recurs, especially when I am in the prayer-meeting. The sister just baptized was the only one of three at all accustomed to attend the prayer-meetings, whilst her age and infirmity necessarily made her attendance irregular. Upon one occasion, having arrived at the place of meeting quite early, I found that none of the members were present. Very soon, however, I noticed the presence of a lady, an intimate friend, who came statedly to hear me preach. I regretted her coming that evening, as I feared that she might be discouraged from repeating her visit. I therefore attempted to persuade her to leave, by telling her that it was "only a prayer-meeting." She replied, "I know it." I then expressed the opinion that there would not be many out. "I do not think that there will be," she answered. I then concluded to let her alone, and found that, for the succeeding ten years that I remained in Providence, she was regular in attendance on the means of grace. In a few weeks after her first visit, I had the pleasure of burying this sister with Christ in baptism, and introducing her to the Christian church, since / which time she has, supported by the grace of God, been a worthy example to believers. From this fact, I learned a lesson. Ever since the first visit of my sister to the prayer-meeting, I have been far more desirous, under all circumstances, to persuade persons to attend, rather than to leave, the house of prayer.

The next month (February) I baptized two, one of whom was my wife—a fact of thrilling interest to the church and congregation, and of comfort and encouragement to myself. The day was one of the coldest of the season. She was an invalid, unable to walk without her crutch and cane. This excited deep interest; and notwithstanding the extreme cold and the distance to the place, yet hundreds went to behold the administration. Many thought the act to be imprudent, whilst others feared the result would be injurious to her already feeble and almost hopeless condition, so far as her bodily health was concerned. But the reverse of this was the fact. She began to improve in health from that day, and was soon able to walk with the aid of her cane only, and even to attend to most of her household duties.

My salary was but three hundred dollars per year while in Providence; and yet the Lord helped me, and raised up friends for me. I speak it with gratitude and thankfulness. Foremost among these were brethren and sisters of the First Church, Rev. Dr. Wayland, Rev. Dr. Granger, Mr. Henry Marchant, Miss Phebe Jackson, Mrs. Joseph Rogers, Mrs. Hope Ives, and Mrs. Samuel G. Arnold. I never appealed to one of them in vain. Most of the assistance which they rendered me was unsolicited. At the outset, one-half of my salary was raised by the church, and the other half appropriated by the Rhode Island State Convention, mostly through the influence of deacon Varnum J. Bates and brother Henry Marchant, who ever proved true and faithful friends to me.

The next month (March) the Lord was pleased to bless our feeble efforts still more, and we baptized into the likeness of Christ's death, five sisters. In the month following, seven more were added by baptism. In the short time of four months, fifteen females were added to the original nine, and some two or three by letter.

When we first commenced, our opponents gave us six months to complete our history, saying that neither the pastor nor people were equal to the work we had undertaken. Nevertheless, we were not discouraged, for we remembered that it was not by might nor by power that the work was to be accomplished, but by the Spirit of God alone.

So we moved on, regardless of all that Satan could say. It was even predicted that we should have to use the females instead of men for officers, as the latter would never join our feeble band, even if converted. This, I confess, caused me some anxiety; but I felt that the battle was the Lord's. The contest, however, appeared to wax hotter and hotter with every aggressive movement we made upon the kingdom of Satan. In less than one year, I baptized eight or ten young men, making about twenty-five added to our membership, thus giving us, in all, thirty-two members. All kinds of stories were in circulation about us, and especially about my preaching, which created much excitement among the people, so that, being induced by curiosity, many were attracted to hear me preach. Some of these came to stay, and became my warmest friends and the ablest contributors to the church until the day of their death.

I will mention one of these as a case in point,

4 D

namely, that of Mrs. Patience Proffitt, an old resident of the city, and, like many others, living upon her morality, thinking herself good enough without attending church. I think this place of worship had been built twenty years, and she told me she had never been to it once. She had heard so much said about me and the church, as to come to the conclusion that I must be indeed a dreadful creature. Her strong desire to hear me, however, overpowered her objections to going to church. She accordingly came, once and again, and yet again. Within four weeks, it was my happiness to baptize her into the fellowship of the church. From that day she pursued a highly consistent course, being constant in her attendance at the house of God, always ready for every good word and work, and contributing most liberally for the support of the pastor and the general expenses of the church—at least twelve dollars per year.

The enemy seeing that he was not only thus foiled, but that he was conferring upon us a real benefit, changed his tactics, and "behold! there was a great calm." Every thing said of us now was by way of commendation; and the world spoke approvingly of our enterprise and success. But this proved to be more injurious to us than any thing we had experienced before. From that day the cause began to wane. Alas! month after month now passed, and none inquired the way to Zion with their faces thitherwards.

We now began to turn our attention to the condition of the material building, which, since its erection, twenty years before, had not received any repairs. We found that it needed painting and thorough renovation, both externally and internally. We proposed to expend some seven hundred dollars upon the house; but the mode of raising the money was difficult to decide. The general superintendence of the whole movement fell to my lot. It devolved upon me to make the contracts, to take a general supervision of the work, to procure the funds, and pay the bills. All this, in addition to my engagements to preach four times in each week, made my labors very arduous. I succeeded in collecting from friends about five hundred and seventy-five dollars, leaving the remainder to be provided by the church. The work occupied some six or eight months, giving us, when completed, one of the best, the neatest, and most commodious places of worship in the city, so much so, that many of the colored people regarded it as quite aristocratic. Notwithstanding the aspersions cast upon myself and the church, it became an acknowledged fact that we were the strongest, and, the most influential body, with the best house of worship of any of the colored churches of Providence. Thus, under God, had we become established with a seeming bright prospect before us. We now numbered sixty-five members. Probably as much was accomplished during the first three years as during the following seven of my pastorate.

I now began to think of making a change. After enjoying the kindness of a large circle of friends, and the confidence of my brethren in the denomination, and having, as I hoped, learned some useful lessons in my ministerial work, and especially in the item of church government, upon consultation with my much esteemed and honored friend, the Rev. Dr. Wayland, I resolved to resign my charge of the Meeting Street Baptist Church of Providence, which resolution was soon executed, and my resignation presented.

I knew not yet, however, whither to turn my steps; but still I trusted in the Lord for direction. My heart being drawn towards Baltimore, I solicited Dr. Wayland to write William Creho, Esq., and ascertain if, in the judgment of his friends it would be expedient to commence a new interest in that city. The answer being that the propriety of such a movement was decidedly doubtful, the plan was immediately abandoned. At this stage, as at other times, I received some wise and kind counsel from the Doctor, which I shall ever remember with gratitude. Would that others would imitate him in showing uniform kindness to their poorer brethren! He gave me good advice. One thing he told me I must never do; that was, not to make, or attempt to make, any important change affecting my own interest, or the interest of the church with which I might be connected, without first taking counsel with the leading brethren in the denomination touching the subject. I hope ever to heed this counsel, for I find there is wisdom in it.

CHAPTER X.

RESIGNATION ACCEPTED—VISIT PHILADELPHIA AND WASH-
INGTON—ACCEPT THE CALL OF THE "SHILOH" BAP-
TIST CHURCH — INSTALLATION—BAPTISM—PREPARA-
TION TO LEAVE FOR ENGLAND—OFFICIAL DOCUMENTS.

IN the early spring of 1848, my resignation of
the pastorate of the church in Providence, ten-
dered six months before, having been accepted,
I was again at liberty, and needed rest. This
however, was denied, as, in less than a month, I
received invitations from Rochester, Washington,
and other places. I immediately declined Rochester, as the Rev. Dr. Church, then the pastor of
the First Baptist Church of that city, who had
held out to me strong inducements to accept the
oversight of the colored church in Rochester, was
about to leave. I accepted, however, the invitation to visit Washington, especially as I had long
desired to go South.

So soon as I could make the necessary arrangements, I started for my destination. Tarrying in
Philadelphia over the Sabbath, I was invited and

consented to preach for the Shiloh Baptist Church, then destitute of a pastor, although without any idea of preaching "on trial." Subsequently, however, a correspondence was opened with me by deacon Westward F. Keeling, who removed from my mind some unfounded prejudices which I had hitherto entertained against the church, after which, brother Keeling suggested that I should again visit them at their expense. After my visit to Washington, I acceded to their request, and preached for them two Sabbaths, having a very pleasant visit, and being very agreeably disappointed by what I saw and heard. After a somewhat lengthened correspondence, extending over two months, I finally considered it to be my duty to accept their "call," with a salary of four hundred dollars. It was agreed, also, that I should proceed to England to solicit funds for the liquidation of their church debt. In less than one year, therefore, from the time of my resigning my position in Providence, I was publicly installed as pastor of the Shiloh Baptist Church, Philadelphia, having also spent some three months or more with the Second Church in Washington, D. C. The installation service was an occasion of deep interest, many of the ministering brethren

of the city taking part in the exercises, and the
Rev. W. L. Dennis, then pastor of the New Market Street Church, preaching the sermon from
2 Cor. iv. 5:—"We preach not ourselves, but
Christ Jesus, the Lord," &c.

The reasons which actuated me to decide upon
this field of labor, in preference to others, were
principally the following:—

1st. The Shiloh Baptist Church occupied the
most substantial and commodious church edifice
in the denomination, occupied by the colored
people in any city of the Union.

2d. On account of pressing liabilities, it was in
danger of passing out of their hands; and

3d. It was situated in the midst of a dense
population who needed the Word of Life.

I felt, therefore, that if at least the building
could be saved, a good work would be effected.
No one doubted my inadequacy for the task more
than myself; but, after mature deliberation and
earnest prayer to God for direction, trusting in
His strength alone, I entered upon my labors.

After about two months' labor with the church,
I returned to my family in Providence to make
preparation for my visit to England, there appearing no alternative but to seek funds abroad.

On my arrival home, my companion, who was still afflicted with the disease in her limbs, and had the care of our two children, appeared averse to my taking such a step, doubting whether, under the circumstances, it was my duty. But believing that I could trust them safely in the hands of our heavenly Father, who is the Helper of the helpless, I soon completed my arrangements, and parted in the full hope of meeting again under a brighter sky.

The next Sabbath, being the third Lord's day in May, I again met with my brethren in Philadelphia, and had the privilege of baptizing three candidates into the fellowship of the church, and of administering the ordinance of the Lord's Supper. We all felt it to be a blessed day, and were much encouraged. Mutual congratulations were made, and a mutual covenant entered into to be more faithful to each other and our Saviour.

The time of departure was fixed for the tenth day of the month following, for which the church commenced to make active preparation. The intervening time was indeed a season of trial, which only those who have had a similar experience can justly appreciate.

A committee of the church having been ap-

4 *

pointed to prepare a letter of appeal to our English brethren, it was presented and adopted on the
twelfth of June. One was also received from the
pastors of the city, and a certificate from his
Honor, the Mayor, a copy of each of which is
here subjoined:—

SHILOH BAPTIST CHURCH, PHILADELPHIA.

PHILADELPHIA, STATE OF PENNSYLVANIA, U. S. A.
June 12, 1849.

*The "*SHILOH*" Baptist Church of Philadelphia, "to the Churches
of the same faith and order, and to all the friends of the Redeemer, in the United Kingdom of Great Britain, Scotland,
and Ireland, send Greeting.*

DEAR BRETHREN: We, the members composing the
"Shiloh Baptist Church," would respectfully and affectionately call the attention of their brethren and friends abroad
to the present condition of their church and finances, and
solicit a share of their kind assistance to enable them to
complete their house of worship.

Our corner-stone was laid on the 29th of September, 1845,
and great and difficult as the work appeared to be, we have
not only succeeded in building a house for the worship of
God, but in raising the sum of *two thousand dollars* towards
the payment of the same.

The balance of four thousand dollars *we still owe*, and have
been called upon, and urged to raise, and our earnest desire
is to be released from the pressure of this obligation. Now,
dear brethren, we call upon you, as the professed friends of
our Lord and Master, to aid us in this laudable effort. The
members of our own "Shiloh," according to their circumstances, have exerted themselves to the very extent of their

abilities; and our friends in this city and elsewhere have afforded us much encouragement and generous aid in the prosecution of our noble enterprise ; therefore, having done what we could at *home*, we resolved, after solemn deliberation and prayer, to go *abroad*, and solicit from friends across the Atlantic, a share of that liberality which we believe they are ever ready cheerfully to exercise to objects of Christian worth.

To this end we have appointed our beloved brother and pastor, Jeremiah Asher, in whom we have all confidence, to travel and visit the churches and brethren in England, Scotland, and Ireland, and lay before them the present condition of our pecuniary obligations, and obtain their free offerings. This brother we would respectfully recommend to you, and refer you to him for all the particulars embraced within the circle of our affairs.

We trust, dear brethren, coming among you as he does, in the name of the Lord and our "Shiloh," that his visit will not be in vain ; that you will not forget, in this instance, "Ethiopia is stretching forth her hands unto God," and that every one of you unto whom application shall be made will give according as he purposeth in his heart.

Done by order and in behalf of the church at a regular church meeting, held on the 12th June, 1849, and signed by

JOHN BROWN, *Church Clerk.*
WESTWARD F. KEELING,
SPENCER MITCHELL,
MOSES WILLIAMS,
MUKES ALMOND,   } *Deacons.*
EDWIN JOHNSON,
ROBERT RUFFIN,

CITY OF PHILADELPHIA,   }
STATE OF PENNSYLVANIA, }

THE undersigned pastors of Baptist churches in the city and county of Philadelphia, State of Pennsylvania, United States of America, beg leave most cordially to recommend the bearer, Rev. Jeremiah Asher, to the confidence and esteem of their brethren in England, to which country he goes, to obtain some aid in paying for a neat and convenient house of worship, which is unfortunately in danger of passing from the possession of the church, unless funds are procured to meet their pressing liabilities. In this new country, claims of this kind are so frequent and pressing, in order to provide religious instruction for the vast numbers of emigrants crowding from the old countries to our shores, that it is impossible for us to meet them all. We feel that we have a sort of claim upon England to aid us in our efforts for the evangelizing of this land, in which so many of her own subjects are finding homes.

J. LANSING BURROWS, Pastor of Broad Street Church, Philadelphia.

JOSEPH BELCHER, late Pastor of Mount Tabor Baptist Church.

B. R. LOXLEY, Schuylkill Branch, First Church, Philada.

THOMAS S. MALCOLM, Cor. Sec. of the American Baptist Publication Society.

W. L. DENNIS, Pastor of New Market Street Baptist Church, Philadelphia.

DANIEL SCOTT, Pastor of the Union Baptist Church.

DANIEL DODGE, Pastor of Second Baptist Church in Philadelphia.

GEORGE B. IDE, Pastor of First Baptist Church, Philadelphia.

A. D. GILLETTE, Pastor of the Eleventh Baptist Church, Philadelphia.

GEORGE J. MILES, Pastor of the Third Baptist Church, Philadelphia.

JOHN A. McKEAN, Pastor of the Second Church, Southwark, Philadelphia.

GEORGE KEMPTON, Pastor of Spruce Street Baptist Ch., Philadelphia.

EDGAR M. LEVY, Pastor of the Baptist Church, West Philadelphia.

PERSONALLY came before me, John Swift, Esq., Mayor of the city of Philadelphia, on this eleventh day of June, Anno Domini one thousand eight hundred and forty-nine, the Rev. A. D. Gillette, who is personally known to me as pastor of one of the Baptist churches of this city, and who acknowledged in my presence that his name, as signed to the annexed recommendation of the Rev. Jeremiah Asher, &c. &c., is in his own proper hand-writing, and that he, the said Rev. Mr. Gillette, was acquainted personally with all the other reverend gentlemen signers thereto, and that their signatures were all genuine, and in their own proper handwritings. In testimony whereof, I have hereto set my hand, and have caused the corporate seal of said city to be affixed the day and year above written.

JOHN SWIFT, *Mayor.*

An effort was now made to raise the necessary funds to defray the expenses of the voyage. This being secured, passage was taken for me on the "Saranak," to sail on the twenty-fifth of June. The fare being paid, but a very small sum remained to pay my first expenses in England.

Verily, I must have been possessed of assurance, or strong faith, to have proceeded with only twenty dollars in my pocket beyond my passage money. But the Lord directed my way, for such were my discouragements on my first arrival in Great Britain, that, had I possessed the means, I should certainly have retraced my steps without seeing much of England, or benefitting "Shiloh." I have since concluded it was well for me and the church that my means were limited to the payment of my passage and some other things which were indispensable to my comfort. But the Lord knows best how to further His own designs, and adapts the means to the end.

CHAPTER XI.

MY DEPARTURE — INCIDENTS OF THE VOYAGE — DEATH AND FUNERAL ON SHIPBOARD—ARRIVAL AT LIVER-POOL—FIRST CONTRIBUTIONS.

I NOW proceed to commence that which I deem to be the most important part of my simple narrative, and give a condensed account of my tour in England, and the progress of my mission.

At noon, on the twenty-fifth day of June, with the thermometer pointing at over one hundred in the shade, accompanied by a large concourse of brethren and sisters, I proceeded to Walnut Street wharf, and embarked on board the sailing-ship "Saranak," bound for Liverpool. After bidding farewell to my dear friends, with a somewhat heavy but hopeful heart, and dropping the tear of friendship, we were soon under way, and in tow by a steamer bound for the Capes. My first movement was to look around upon my fellow-passengers who were to be the companions of my voyage. These I found to be forty in number, four being in the first cabin, eight (including myself) in the second cabin, and the remainder in the steerage.

Our starting was indeed promising. The cool breeze was delightful, and the prospect of a prosperous voyage was good. We supposed that we were not long to continue in tow. And so it happened, for the second day we commenced to beat out by the Capes, the winds being "ahead." Previous to parting company with the steamer, however, a singular circumstance occurred, which I consider to be worth relating, as being one of novelty. We had in company the ship "Thomas H. Perkins," which was for a while towed by the same tug. On board of the "Perkins" was a brother of one of our own passengers. Both had families, and proposed to exchange a visit. No sooner, however was the proposition carried into effect, than the ships parted their lines; the brothers were separated, husbands and wives, fathers and children, until they arrived in Liverpool. The annoyance and sorrow resulting from such a catastrophe can be better imagined than described.

I was now to enter fairly upon "a life on the ocean wave." The experience of the first few days, however, did not dishearten me. But I very soon found that I was doomed to that scourge of the ocean—sea-sickness. However essential to a landsman this may be for an experience of ocean life, I cannot but pronounce it as very far from being pleasant. Previous to leaving land, I had intended to devote much time to reading and writing; but now I found myself to be entirely incapacitated for any such exercises. In fact, I had no disposition either to do or to enjoy anything.

One of our number in the second cabin was an invalid passenger, by the name of Brooks, the son of a widow, and returning home, apparently, to die. I could not but take an interest in his case, and therefore offered him all the assistance which it might be in my power to render. When this sea-sickness assailed me, I could not but feel doubly aggrieved, as I was unable to give him any aid or comfort.

But little occurred during the whole voyage to destroy its monotony. We had the usual changes of calm and storm, of wind and rain, and of standing still and making progress, which is the almost invariable experience of those "who go down to the sea in ships." Having these opportunities to view the wondrous power of Almighty God, and the stupendous majesty of the waters

2 D

which He holds in the hollow of His hand, I could not but be grieved by noticing, in contrast, the card-playing and profanity which so much prevailed on board. From the captain downwards, by the larger number, the name of the Lord was constantly taken in vain.

Let me return to young Brooks. It appeared evident, from the commencement, that he could not survive the voyage. On this account, I became intensely anxious concerning his spiritual condition. I therefore sought an early opportunity to converse with him on the subject of religion; and although I afterwards learned that years before he had professed conversion, yet I found that he had but very indistinct ideas of the requirements of the Gospel, and the depravity of the human heart. From time to time, I conversed and prayed with him, and read the Holy Scriptures to him. Upon one of these occasions, when we had been at sea nearly a month, I had a most pleasing interview with him. I could not but notice that his bodily strength was fast failing, and although I felt that he would never be any better in this world, I began to entertain a hope that, in the world to come, he would receive life everlasting. On this day, (July 20,) during the forenoon, he called me to his berth, and expressed a wish that I would read to him, and converse and pray with him. I read the eleventh chapter of the Gospel by John, and endeavored to explain to him the great truths therein contained. I then poured out my soul to God on his behalf, when it seemed as if he could not contain himself any longer, and broke forth in strains of gratitude to God for His unbounded goodness. "His mercy o me is very great," said he. "Oh, how I thank God that my lot has been cast here with one who can pray for me, and direct me in the way everlasting!" I then tried to commend him to the Lord, and I could not but feel that the Lord was with us. My friend seemed to have the spirit of prayer in his heart, and I can have no doubt but that it was said of him from that time, "Behold, he prayeth!" He appeared to give himself unreservedly to the Lord, and to trust for salvation in the atonement effected by Jesus Christ. How thankful I was that so great a privilege should be mine! that the honor of pointing a fellow-man to the Lamb of God, who taketh away the sins of the world, should be conferred upon one so unworthy! I felt that if the Lord would only make me the agent to lead this young man to Christ, I should be more than amply compensated for all the deprivations which I was enduring. At the close of our interview, he requested me to take the name and residence of his mother, that, should he not survive the voyage, and I should visit Bristol, where she lived, I might communicate to her the particulars of his last hours.

On the following day, I found him still more reduced in strength, and evidently sinking quite rapidly. We endeavored to make him comfortable; but such were the inconveniences under which we labored in the second cabin, that the task was futile. He apparently became fully reconciled to his condition. We believed that his sins were forgiven, and therefore felt to rejoice in the God of his salvation. His relation of experience was so clear to my mind, as to leave no doubt but that he had previously, at the time of his professed conversion in Jersey, known something of the renewing influences of the Holy Spirit. "But," said he, "I soon went back again into the world, in pursuit of its pleasures. Yet the good Lord has again brought me to see what He had done for me, to feel my ingratitude, and to seek forgiveness for my sins." Then he again broke forth in utterances of gratitude to God, that

his lot had been cast with me, and, rising up,
implored that the blessing of God might rest upon
me, my mission, and people. A more earnest
prayer I do not remember ever to have heard.
May the Lord grant an abundant answer! Although I have but little confidence in death-bed
repentances generally, there are, doubtless, some
that are genuine, thus displaying the power of
sovereign grace.

A few days after, (July 27,) I found that my
young friend was very near his end. During the
day, when several were on the deck fishing, we
were summoned to see him die. He appeared to
be in the last struggle; but it proved to be only
the breaking of an abscess, the discharge of which
was so rapid and copious as to threaten strangu-
lation. After this, he rallied for a while, but soon
swooned away, and, at about nine o'clock in the
evening, breathed his last without a struggle.

The utmost confusion now prevailed. An
inventory was taken of his effects, and the ship's
carpenter immediately commenced to sew up the
body, together with the clothing which he wore
when he died, in a piece of canvas. It was
indeed a solemn sight to see one so prepared for
burial in the mighty waters.

And now a funeral at sea! Those who have never seen one must utterly fail to realize its solemnity. At eight o'clock on the following morning, we were summoned to the burial. The body having been previously prepared, and a heavy weight attached to the feet, it was placed on a plank, and carried to the lee gangway, where the passengers and crew assembled. The captain performed the service, reading from the church prayer-book the form designated for use on such occasions; and then the body was committed to the deep, in the hope of a glorious resurrection. I felt sad at heart. The profanity of the captain and many others on board, card-playing on the very table whereon laid the form of my deceased friend but a few hours ago, not only showed me how depraved is the natural heart, but led me to pray more fervently that this dispensation of the providence of God might be sanctified to all.

Apart from this melancholy incident, nothing of special interest occurred during the whole voyage. The time was long, and the passage tedious. The thirtieth of July was my last day at sea on my outward bound passage. This I endeavored to improve by presenting my object to the passengers, who generously encouraged me with a subscription, which, although small, was an earnest of the success with which, by the blessing of God, I was destined to meet in Great Britain. On the afternoon of the twenty-ninth, after being at sea thirty-two days, and seeing no land, the captain told us we would see the light at Hollyhead at eleven o'clock that night. At ten o'clock, a man was sent aloft, and at one the light was cried. Next day, we took the pilot, and soon our journey was at an end.

CHAPTER XII.

ARRIVAL IN LIVERPOOL—CONSULTATION WITH MINIS-
TERS—VISIT LONDON—LEAVE FOR BRISTOL—POST-
PONEMENT OF EFFORT—PROCEED TO CHELTENHAM—
THENCE TO BIRMINGHAM—COMMENCEMENT OF SUC-
CESS.

AFTER thirty-six days spent at sea, it was my
privilege, on July 31, to set my feet on dry land,
and to thank the Lord for that rich goodness
which had followed me all the voyage through.
Having arrived in port at twelve o'clock on the
night of the 30th, we did not land until eight
on the following morning, when it was to view
one of the largest commercial cities of Great
Britain. As my object is not description, I shall
not attempt a picture of Liverpool. Suffice it to
say, that whilst it is one of the finest seaports of
the island, one may see there the extremes of
wealth and poverty, of virtue and vice. The
immense number of shipping in the harbor, with
the long and magnificent blocks of warehouses on
the quays, impress a foreigner favorably as to the
immense value of the commerce of England.

Whilst on the other hand, the open wickedness and profligacy visible on every side, cannot fail to pain the heart of every Christian philanthropist.

My first business, after having provided myself with comfortable lodgings, was to seek out the Baptist clergymen, that I might represent my case, and take counsel with them as to the most desirable course to pursue. After consultation with the Rev. Messrs. James Lister, Charles M. Birrell, and Hugh S. Brown, the two former of them treated me with special kindness, and after examining my papers, advised me to proceed direct to London, that city being, as Mr. Birrell suggested, the "headquarters" of the empire.

On the morning, therefore, of Saturday, the fourth of August, I started for the great metropolis, where I arrived in safety on the evening of the same day, after one of the most delightful rides I had ever enjoyed. The scenery in every direction was sublime. Never had I beheld a country, for so long a distance, in so high a state of cultivation. On my arrival, I proceeded at once to a boarding-house kept by a deacon of the New Park Street Church, formerly under the pastoral care of Drs. Gill and Rippon, and now under that of the celebrated Rev. Charles H. Spurgeon,

5 E

Rev. C. M. Birrell having given me a kind letter
of introduction. There I found a home indeed. /\

The following day, being the Sabbath, after the
devotion of the morning, in which I was requested
to read the 84th Psalm, and lead in prayer, I accepted the invitation of my brother to accompany
him to church, and listen to his pastor, the Rev,
James Smith, Mr. Spurgeon's immediate prede-
cessor. I felt that I could most sincerely say,
with the sweet singer of Israel, "I was glad when
they said unto me, Let us go up unto the house
of the Lord," six weeks having elapsed since I
had enjoyed an opportunity to attend upon the
services of the sanctuary. In the morning, the
pastor preached a most excellent discourse from
the 26th verse of the 17th chapter of the Gospel
by St. John—"I have declared unto them thy
name, and will declare it: that the love wherewith
thou hast loved me may be in them, and I in
them." I listened again in the evening to the
same preacher, who discoursed from the 31st verse
of the 5th chapter of Judges—"So let all thine
enemies perish, O Lord; but let them that love
him be as the sun when he goeth forth in his
might." This, I think, was one of the best sermons to which I ever listened. After the service,

the ordinance of the Lord's Supper was administered, when I was introduced to the church as a
Baptist minister from Philadelphia, and invited to
a seat at the Lord's table. I could truly say that
it was good to be there. "How amiable are thy
tabernacles, O Lord of hosts!"

My object was now to make myself and my
mission known to the leading ministers of London. On Monday, therefore, I proceeded in quest
of the Rev. William Groser, then the editor of the
Baptist Magazine, to whom I had brought letters
of introduction. I was privileged to meet him, in
company with other ministers, at the Missionary
Rooms, in Moorgate Street. They examined my
credentials, expressed themselves satisfied, but discouraged me from making any attempt to raise
funds in London for the present, giving me, at the
same time, the following certificate, and advised
me to go into the country, and remain there until
the fall.

"33 MOORGATE STREET, LONDON.
August 6, 1849.

"We have examined Mr. Asher's documents, which are
respectfully signed, and we hope that those philanthropical
gentlemen who take a lively interest in the welfare of the
colored people of the United States will deem this a case
deserving of their aid.

"We are decidedly of the opinion that Mr. Asher had better postpone his calls in London for six or eight weeks.

JOSEPH ANGUS,
FREDERICK TRESTRAIL,
WILLIAM GROSER,
EDWARD STEANE, D. D.

The principal reason of the advise contained in the recommendation was on account of the prevalence of the cholera in the city, in consequence of which, a large number of the principal families had retired to the country. The ravages of this disease were at this time truly alarming. It was quite common to see the poorer classes of people carrying their dead upon their shoulders to the last resting-place. More than once I witnessed two men carrying a coffin to the graveyard, whilst perhaps the wife, daughter, or sister of the deceased was the only mourner! Verily, indeed, was I made to feel that "in the midst of life we are in death."

Finding that I could not obtain a hearing from the people, I proceeded immediately to Bristol, hoping and praying for better success, and desiring to see Mrs. Brooks, the mother of the young man who had died on board the "Saranak." I could not fail to be amazed at the antiquated appearance of the city. It was certainly the most so of any which I had visited in all my travels. My first call was upon the widowed mother of my deceased friend, who received me with great kindness and many fervent expressions of gratitude, having been referred to me for the particulars of her son's death by the captain of the ship. Being introduced by her to the Rev. George H. Davis, one of the leading Baptist ministers of the city, I was again discouraged by his informing me that there was but little hope of a favorable presentation of my case. He was kind enough, however, to invite me to accompany him to a public meeting of the Bristol Society for the Promotion of Christianity among the Jews, and to offer to introduce me to the audience as one of the speakers. I willingly accepted the invitation, as I had not previously been permitted to address an English congregation. When, in the course of the evening, my name was announced, I was received with almost deafening applause. I addressed the assembly for about fifteen minutes, and then took my seat amid the greatest enthusiasm. The die was cast. The Rev. Thomas Winter immediately espoused my cause, and, with the Rev. Evan Probert, recommended me to visit Cheltenham and Birmingham, and return to Bristol early in September, promising me that the subject should have due consideration.

Acting upon the advice of these ministering brethren, I proceeded to Cheltenham, but only again to meet with disappointment, as a missionary from Jamaica had but just left, after making collections. I found that I could do no less than extend my journey to Birmingham without loss of time. I was assured, however, by the Rev. Mr. Lewis, that at an early day he would inform me, and I should come and see what his people would do for me. There I was very kindly received by the Rev. Thomas Swan, to whom I had delivered a letter of introduction from his old and familiar friend, the late Rev. Dr. Belcher, of Philadelphia. However, in common with ministering brethren in other places, he was apparently much perplexed as to the course it would be desirable for me to pursue, so many objects of Christian benevolence being already before the people. As the following day would be the Sabbath, he invited me to preach for him, which I readily assented to. After delivering an excellent sermon in the morning, he read to his people Dr. Belcher's letter of introduction, stated the object of my mission, and warmly commended me to the sympathies and benevolence of the friends generally, and gave notice that I would preach in the afternoon. I began to feel quite encouraged, and thanked the Lord that he was now opening a door for me. In the afternoon of the same day, I endeavored to preach from these words: "If any of you lack wisdom, let him ask of God, that giveth to all men liberally, and upbraideth not; and it shall be given him." (James i. 5.) I felt that the Lord was with me of a truth. After the sermon, I presented my case, which appeared to make a favorable impression. From this time, and during all my stay in Birmingham, I was most cordially invited to partake of the hospitalities of the brethren.

On the following Tuesday evening, I was introduced into a gathering which was entirely new to me, and which I believe to be almost exclusively English, being a "tea-party," to which an admission fee was charged. It was called a Meeting of Thanksgiving to God for his blessing in enabling them to pay off a debt on a house at one of the village preaching stations. I was invited to address the meeting, and plead for the Shiloh Church, as the result of which I realized about fifteen dollars.

On Thursday evening, I again preached to the same congregation, using for my text the 13th verse of the 103d Psalm—"Like as a father pitieth his children, so the Lord pitieth them that fear Him"—when I endeavored to impress my hearers with a sense of the paternal goodness of God. And surely His goodness was manifested to me, for I found, at the close of the week, by direct and indirect application, that I had collected about one hundred dollars.

I cannot leave Birmingham without recording, with extreme thankfulness, the great kindness which I received from the Rev. Thomas Swan and family. He generously spent his time for two or three days in going with me from house to house, and, when unable to accompany me in person, sent his daughter to introduce me to the people. May the blessing of the Lord, which maketh rich, and addeth no sorrow therewith, ever rest upon him and his dear family! Also deacon John Walters, who kindly furnished me with lodging and the comforts of home during my stay in that city, and a host of kind friends, all of whom deserve my lasting gratitude.

My next engagement was at King's Norton, where I preached a sermon founded on Zech.

xii. 1, and collected a small sum; and after visiting Astwood Bank, and walking twenty miles, I
again reached Birmingham. Here, still alive to
my work, I called upon a wealthy Episcopalian,
whose heart and purse I had prayed the Lord to
open. He inquired if I was a preacher. I told
him I tried to preach. He received me kindly,
gave me ten dollars, and thanked me for calling
upon him. He said any man who would preach
Christ, he would help him, even if he was not of the
same denomination as himself. Then, after a brief
visit to Dudley, where I preached on the first Sabbath in September, I returned to Birmingham,
which city I left for Bristol on the following day,
with a heart full of gratitude to God for all my
travelling mercies, and hopeful of new success.

5 *

CHAPTER XIII.

ON my return to Bristol, finding that a City
Missionary Meeting was in session at Hope Chapel,
Clifton, composed of the different denominations,
I immediately started for that place, in order to
lay my case before the ministers. They received
me kindly, gave me a recommendation to their
friends, and a certificate of the genuineness of my
testimonials. This was signed by the Rev. Messrs.
Thomas S. Crisp, George Wood, Thomas Porter,
George H. Davis, John Jack, D. Thomas, Nathan-
iel Haycroft, Thomas Winter, Evan Probert, and
Henry I. Roper. My stay in Bristol was protracted to about four weeks. Meanwhile, I was
quite successful in the city and vicinity, and enjoyed many delightful seasons with the people of

God. It was my privilege, soon after my arrival, to preach in the Broadmead Baptist Chapel, made notable by the eloquence of Robert Hall. I felt my unworthiness in attempting to address such a congregation; but, leaning on the Lord's promise, "As thy day, so shall thy strength be," I felt to be sustained by His gracious power, and enjoyed the service, and many of the saints seemed comforted. I also preached at North Bradley, Ashton, at the King Street Chapel, and Pit Hay, besides addressing several public meetings and tea-parties.

My visit to Ashton being invested with very much of personal interest, deserves more than a passing notice. My time there was principally spent with the Rev. Mr. Brown, a Presbyterian minister, for whom I preached twice on the Sabbath. My text in the morning was the 24th verse of the 31st Psalm—"Be of good courage, and He shall strengthen your heart, all ye that hope in the Lord." In the evening, I selected a part of the 37th verse of the 6th chapter of the Gospel by John—"Him that cometh to me, I will in no wise cast out." "What a mercy," said one of the congregation, "that those words are in the Bible!" Blessed words, indeed, are they, from which we may derive comfort in every time of perplexity and distress!

Through the kindness of one of the deacons of the Presbyterian church, I received an invitation to visit Ashton Court, the residence of the late Sir John Smith. This was esteemed to be one of the most splendid palaces in all England, and had then fallen into the possession of an aged widowed sister of Sir John's. Having accepted the invitation, I addressed a note to the lady, making an appointment, but found, to my regret, on fulfilling my engagement, that she was unable to be seen, on account of sickness. She, however, sent me a liberal subscription, with an invitation to go through the entire building, which I understood would occupy the whole day. I learned that the lady was a pious member of the church of England, and that most of her retinue of servants were members of different denominations. Here I found Presbyterians, Methodists, and Baptists, but all "one in Jesus Christ." One of the rooms of this elegant mansion was fitted up as a chapel, with a very large organ, and all the necessary furniture for a place of worship. Here it was the custom of her ladyship and servants to assemble morning and night for prayers. She herself would announce the hymns to be sung, and the butler, who was a Baptist, would read the Scriptures, and sometimes lead in the devotions. Happy, indeed, must be such a family. Greatly did I rejoice to find such piety prevailing to some extent among the English aristocracy. I happily learned after-wards that this was by no means an isolated instance.

One of the most pleasing sights of the morning was a view from a window of the magnificent dining-room, of a large herd of deer, consisting of between three and four hundred, skipping about, as the wise man says, "like a roe upon the moun-tains." A glance at so beautiful a park, and such a scene of innocent life, I never expect to be-hold again.

As I was able to spend only about three hours in the inspection of this mansion, I was forced to leave much unseen; but I had seen sufficient to form strong impressions of its grandeur, and the lavish expenditure which had been incurred, year after year, for its support. Yet I could not refrain from thinking of the Saviour's declaration—"In my Father's house are many mansions," and for a moment, in imagination, comparing it with those

which my Lord had gone to prepare for all who
love His appearing.

Near the close of my visit in Bristol, it was my
privilege, in company with the Rev. Mr. Haycroft, to attend a public meeting, at the King
Street Chapel, for the reception of the delegates
who had been appointed to the Peace Congress in
Paris. Mr. Haycroft presided over the large and
respectable assembly, and called upon me to make
a speech, introducing me as his "friend and brother," a Baptist minister of the United States of
America. I at first declined to speak upon such
an occasion ; but, when he quoted Lord Nelson
at Trafalgar, "England expects every man this
day to do his duty," the tumultuous applause of
the audience was irresistible. I endeavored to
say a few words on the occasion, and, by the advice of my friend, briefly introduced the object of
my mission, which was received with favor.

From an early part of my visit, I found Mr.
Haycroft to be one of my firmest friends and best
helpers. A young man of fine talent and com-
manding ability, I could not fail to regard him as
a worthy successor to the celebrated Robert Hall,
as pastor of the Broadmead Baptist Church.

My stay in Bristol will be remembered by me

as one of the most pleasant which I enjoyed in
England. From ministers, deacons, and church-
members alike, I received almost unbounded kindness. Their hospitality was perfectly free, whilst
upon several occasions I was invited to dine with
select parties. Upon one of these, at the house of
Mr. Wm. Warren, in company with the Rev. Mr.
Crisp, President of Bristol College; Rev. Messrs.
Haycroft and Davis, Dr. Chandler, Mr. Morcom,
and some others, I had the happiness of meeting
the widow of the late Robert Hall, one evening,
after preaching, when she politely invited me to
take tea with her. She is one of the most refined
ladies in England—an introduction which I remember with unfeigned interest. Thus was I
treated in Bristol and throughout England generally. When will America answer the appeal,
" Am I not a man and a brother?"

" Am I *not man*, by sin and suffering tried?
Am I *not man*, for whom the Saviour died?"

From Bristol I went to Trowbridge, Frome,
Bath, and Cheltenham, designing to spend a few
days in the latter place, where I received the cordial recommendations of the Revs. W. G. Lewis
and A. Morton Brown. Cheltenham is one of the

most popular watering-places in England. Besides my opportunities to collect donations, I had, also, numerous invitations to preach the Gospel. Being invited, on one occasion, to occupy the pulpit of the Rev. Mr. Lewis, I found convened, at the time appointed, one of the largest audiences I had yet addressed. I do not suppose that there could have been less than fifteen hundred or two thousand persons present. I felt that the Lord was again with me, and realized more than ever the force of His promise—" Lo! I am with you alway, even to the end of the world!"

At Gloucester, I was privileged to see the monument erected to the Bishop of Gloucester, who, very many years ago, was burnt for his adherence to the doctrines of Christ. This, with the ancient cathedral, appeared to be nearly all deserving public notice as objects of antiquity.

Going thence by way of Cheltenham, in the course of a few hours, I found myself in the rich old city of Oxford, one of the English seats of classic learning, and made memorable by some of the religious annals of the past. The splendor of this city fairly surprised me. Piles of magnificent architecture filled the eye wheresoever it turned.

Its colleges, of which there seemed to be about twenty, are beautiful specimens of the art of the architect and builder. But the most remarkable sight was in connection with the martyrdom of some bishops of olden time, being a splendid monument erected to their honor. I visited the room wherein they were tried and condemned, and the very spot where the stake stood to which they were bound, and where they were burned, that being marked by a cross in the pavement. The reformers to whom I refer are Ridley, Latimer, and Cranmer, who died bearing testimony to their Saviour, and whose names will ever occupy a high niche in the temple of Christian fame. I pray God that their memory and their works may be revered by the Christian world to the end of time!

As it forms no part of my design, however, to attempt the task of description, I shall pass on with the brief review of my labors. On the evening of my first Sabbath in Oxford, I was privileged to preach to a large congregation in the pulpit statedly occupied by the Rev. Mr. Bryan, but with very little comfort to myself, as I was in poor health, and not a little embarrassed by occupying such a position. The friends, however,

E 2

insisted upon my preaching again on the following evening, which I did with far more freedom, and, I trust, profit to my hearers. The following Thursday evening, I endeavored to proclaim the truth, as it is in Jesus, at Abington, after which, I returned to Oxford, where I received some "material aid." Here, also, I was the recipient of much kindness at the hands of Joseph Warne, Esq., whom I found in every respect to be the Christian gentleman, and occupying the position of post-master of Oxford—a strong friend to the colored man.

My next journey was to Leamington (a tedious ride of five or six hours by stage-coach), where I was most kindly and hospitably entertained by the Rev. Octavius Winslow. As this gentleman is so well known in America, through his works, I append the following graceful recommendation which he gave me to be presented to his friends:—

"From a personal acquaintance with several of the ministers of the United States, who have signed the Rev. Mr. Asher's testimonials, I have every confidence in him as a Christian minister; and from the deeply interesting character of his church, I most cordially commend his case to the Christian benevolence of *all* who love the Lord Jesus Christ in sincerity.   OCTAVIUS WINSLOW.

Leamington, Oct. 27, 1849."

Mr. Winslow extended to me great kindness. He not only gave me the above recommendation and a donation, but procured me comfortable lodgings, defraying the expenses from his own purse. He also invited me to take a seat at his own table, whenever it might be convenient with my other arrangements. Although unable, on account of ill health, to yield to his urgent request and preach to his people on the Sabbath, I addressed them in the prayer-meeting on the Monday evening following, and afterwards received from them a liberal contribution. I collected, in all, about sixty-five dollars. At Leamington, as in every other place, I was treated with the greatest kindness and that reception which Englishmen know so well how to extend to strangers. My indisposition was now such, that by the suggestion of a lady who felt a deep interest in my welfare and mission, I was induced to seek the advice of a celebrated physician, who had lately arrived from London, and retired to private life, but charged for giving advice, the money to pay which charges she gave me. After a thorough examination, he assured me that one of my lungs was inflamed, and that, therefore, it was my duty to refrain a while from public speaking, hinting, also, at the probability that it might be necessary for me to return to my own country sooner than I had anticipated. Notwithstanding this advice, I attended, a day or two afterwards, two meetings of the British and Foreign Bible Society, which were held at Warwick, a few miles distant. I was able only, however, to speak briefly at one of them. Leaving Warwick and Leamington with all the dear friends I had made, and whom I may never see more in this world, I proceeded on my travels, having Birmingham first in view, in order to lay by a few days, and, if possible, recruit my almost wasted health, and pay a visit to kind friends there, who had invited me whenever opportunity would allow, while I was in the country, to spend a few days with them, especially if unwell; to be sure to come home, as they styled it, and refresh myself, which I felt very thankful for, and always enjoyed these second benefits.

CHAPTER XIV.

RETURN TO BIRMINGHAM—NEWS FROM HOME—LIVER-
POOL—KINDLY GREETINGS—ROCHDALE AND ASHTON-
UNDER-TYNE.

CONDUCTED by the goodness of God, I was
again permitted to see Birmingham and the dear
family of Mr. John Walters, with whom I had
resided on my previous visit. Under date, Nov. 1,
I find the following paragraph in my diary, which
I quote (although it was never designed for any
other eyes than my own), as showing some of the
peculiar thoughts and emotions which stirred my
soul. "To-day, my health is a little improved.
This may arise partly from the fact that I have
received letters from home and from my dear
church. This was the first time I had heard from
home since my arrival in England. Oh, how
cheering is the intelligence they convey respecting my family and the people of my charge. The
good Lord has mercifully preserved them from
the ravages of disease, for which I desire to be
unceasingly grateful. But the letters bring me,

also, some sad news concerning some whom I left behind, when I came to this country—among others, a fellow-laborer in the Gospel, the Rev. Thomas U. Allen, who is now asleep in Jesus. High expectations had been formed about him. With many others, I had anticipated that, when he should have completed his course of study, he would shine as a bright star in our denomination. But alas! alas! whilst man may propose, God disposes. How unaccountable is this Providence! Truly, "God moves in a mysterious way!" Could the dear brother have foreseen how near was his end, he certainly would not have discontinued preaching to enter college, but would rather have preached Christ with increased earnestness, and to to the last hour of his life would have spent his breath in warning sinners to repent. But he is gone, and his eloquent tongue lies silent in the grave. Never, from henceforth, will I recommend a minister of Jesus Christ to quit the field of labor to obtain an education, however desirable such may appear. May God enable me to learn, from this dispensation, my own mortality! Oh, that my days may be altogether spent in the Lord's service, that my efforts may be abundantly blessed, and that my preaching may be accompanied with the demonstration of the Spirit and with power!"

Having been informed at Leamington that, if I desired to collect anything in Liverpool during the winter, I must go immediately, I resolved to visit that city again without further delay. On my arrival, I found that the cholera had been doing its deadly work. Among others, I learned to my grief, that it had stricken down my friend and brother in Christ, Mr. Fishbourne, at whose house I had made my home during my first visit. This was the second of my landlords who had fallen victims to that scourge. Here, again, I received marked kindness from the resident pastors of different evangelical denominations. I was favored, also, with strong recommendations over the signatures of the Rev. Messrs. Charles M. Birrel, James Lister, Hugh S. Brown, John Stent, Hugh Crichton, William Graham, and Rev. Dr. Raffles. Although my success in this city was not so great as I had anticipated, yet I felt that I had received much from the Lord's stewards for which to be grateful.

After completing my work in Liverpool, I left for Manchester, with a letter of introduction to the Rev. Francis Tucker, who received me with much cordiality. Having heard of me in other parts of the kingdom, he was anxious to see me. He invited me to attend a meeting of the Evangelical Alliance, at the residence of a wealthy brother, who was a member of his church, where, he assured me, I should meet with representatives from all the evangelical denominations of the city. I therefore accompanied him, when he very kindly introduced me to the brethren, and commended my cause to their Christian liberality. Being solicited to address the meeting, I spoke at some length, and so far succeeded in making a favorable impression as to receive several invitations from gentlemen to call at their places of business next day; and those who did not, I took the liberty to invite myself. Previous, however, to commencing my active visitation, I received the following recommendation from the Rev. Mr. Tucker and the Rev. Dr. Halley:—

"MANCHESTER, *Dec.* 7, 1849.

"No testimonials could be more satisfactory than those Mr. Asher brings with him. We very cordially commend his case to the Christians and philanthropists of Manchester.   FRANCIS TUCKER,
                                              ROBERT HALLEY."

Mr. Tucker took a deep interest in me and the object which I represented. After preaching on the Sabbath morning following, he introduced me to his congregation, which is reputed to be one of the most wealthy among the Baptists of England. He then read my testimonials, made some comments, and announced me to preach in the evening. I filled the appointment with comfort to myself, and, I judge, to the satisfaction of the congregation, as I was urgently requested to preach again during the week. My subscription was headed by the gentleman at whose house I attended the meeting on my first arrival, W. R. Callender, Esq., with five pounds, followed by S. B. Hunt, Esq., of New York, and then by W. R———, Esq., with whom I had previously met, under very different circumstances, a short time before, in Liverpool.

I had been directed to call at a certain house, to solicit of the lady residing there a contribution. Doing so, I was accosted at the door by a gentleman, who inquired my business. On communicating to him my errand, he replied that they never subscribed to such objects, and appeared to be absolutely disgusted at the very idea of building churches. He treated me with such apparent
6 F

contempt, that I felt quite relieved when our interview was ended. I turned away discouraged and
disheartened. Very much, therefore, to my surprise, this gentleman was almost the foremost of
those who spoke with me after preaching my first
sermon in Manchester. He immediately extended
to me the hospitalities of his house; but having
already made other arrangements, I could not
accept of his proffered kindness. Nothing less
would satisfy him than my consent to dine with
him on the following day. Upon arriving at his
house (such as King Cotton's subjects usually
occupy), he commenced to apologize for his ungen-
tlemanly and unchristian conduct to me in Liverpool, and, confessing with shame and confusion,
besought my forgiveness, and that I would make
no mention of the matter either to his wife or
pastor. He then gave me a liberal subscription
for my object, and a small sum for my private
purse, besides a general invitation to partake of
dinner or supper at his house at any time during
my stay in Manchester.

My welcome in that city was not confined to
the Baptists. I preached in many of the places
of worship occupied by other denominations of
Christians, and addressed one of the largest Sab-

bath-schools I have ever seen, numbering about two thousand scholars; and all my appeals met with a liberal response. My labors there were both pleasant and remunerative. The list of the names of my Manchester friends I still cherish as a treasure, recalling, even after this lapse of time, their noble generosity.

From Manchester I went to Rochdale, where I also found favor. The Rev. Mr. Burchell received me in the most affectionate manner, and treated me with that attention which I so much needed, after having overworked myself during the previous four weeks spent in the former city. Upon my arrival in town, I engaged rooms at a hotel; but when I called upon Henry Kellsall, Esq., father-in-law of Samuel Peto, Esq., an M. P. for the city of London, he extended me an invitation to make his residence my home during all my stay in Rochdale. This I gladly accepted. An appointment had been made for me to preach on the following Sabbath evening, to Mr. Burchell's congregation, of which Mr. Kellsall's family were members; but owing to a severe cold, which almost entirely destroyed my speech, I feared, at the time, that it would be impossible for me to fulfil my engagement. But, by the specially kind treatment of Mrs. Kellsall, and as the result of the remedies used, I partially recovered my voice. The weather being exceedingly inclement, I was taken to the chapel in their carriage, and succeeded in preaching a short discourse to a very attentive audience. Afterwards, I so far recovered as to be able to attend every meeting held in Mr. Burchell's chapel during my stay in Rochdale. From the friends universally, I received the utmost kindness, but from none so much as from my host and hostess, whose many favors I can never reciprocate. They not only entertained me handsomely, and contributed with true liberality to the fund for the Shiloh Church, but presented me with many valuable articles of clothing for my family, which are still in use. During my stay with them, for about ten days, it fell to my lot to read the Scriptures, and lead in the family devotions, morning and evening, Mr. Kellsall remarking that whenever a minister of Christ lodged beneath his roof, he invariably gave him that portion of the work to perform, and he could not make me an exception.

My next journey was to Ashton-under-Lyne, where, receiving but little pecuniary assistance, although a welcome reception, I remained but two or three days, and then retraced my steps to Rochdale, as I had a standing invitation to stop at Mr. Kellsall's whenever I might again visit that place.

A single circumstance connected with my mission in Manchester ought not to be omitted in this chapter. Soon after my arrival there, I became acquainted with the Sheriff. He was deeply interested in me and the cause which I represented. He said I must raise, in Manchester, five hundred dollars; and he never relaxed his effort until that sum was reached, and in every possible way sought to further my interest by making individual application to his personal friends. No man in England rendered me more important aid than the Sheriff of Manchester.

CHAPTER XV.

AFTER spending a few more days in Rochdale, to pick up "the fragments which remained," I wended my way to Bacup, about seven miles south of the former place. Not having an opportunity to see the Rev. Mr. Dawson at his residence, and learning that he was with his Bible-class at the chapel, I proceeded thither. Arriving at the building, I entered and took a seat with the class. They had not heard of me; and I presume that if an unitiated person had clandestinely found his way into a meeting of some secret society, there could not have been more excitement. I had intended to have sat quietly through the proceedings, and then introduce myself to the pastor, but this was rendered impossible. The minister, finding that he could not secure the attention of the members of his class under the circumstances,

126

then approached me, saying, "I perceive you are a stranger"—a plain truth, which I readily ac-knowledged.

"From what part of the world have you come?" he inquired.

I answered: "From the United States of America.

"Are you a fugitive slave?"

"No."

"May I ask, then, the object of your visit to this country?"

After giving him the information which he sought, he determined not to pursue his usual course that evening, and requested me to address them. This I did for a short time, at the close of which he announced that I would preach in the chapel on the next Lord's day, which service I performed before a large and attentive congre-gation, and, I trust, not without good effect. In the afternoon of the same day, I preached in the Ebenezer Baptist Chapel, and in the evening at Water-barne. The congregations in these differ-ent places were about as large as any I had seen among the Baptists. I collected, in that vicinity, about one hundred dollars.

One little incident in connection with my arrival at Bacup, trivial though it may appear, I must not forbear to mention, especially as the party to whom I refer afterwards emigrated to America. At the close of the meeting to which allusion has been made, Mr. Dawson introduced me to a young man to conduct me to the Temperance Hotel, which was kept, I believe, by one of the members of his church. As the house was quite full, I was recommended to a lodging-house, where I again found that every room was pre-occupied, and thence to another, where a large number of colliers and other laborers were lodging. We effected an entrance by going down a very dirty and narrow pair of steps. The interior presented the most disorderly domestic scene I had ever witnessed, and I therefore very speedily determined that, in the event of their consenting to accommodate me, to find some plausible excuse for not remaining. Upon my conductor inquiring whether I could be accommodated, the landlady replied in the affirmative. Thinking that, perchance, I might be able to find some ground for objection, I made inquiries as to her charges, to which she answered, that depended upon what I wanted. She then inquired if I desired to occupy a bed alone, when I replied, "Yes; for I do not suppose that any of your boarders would care to lodge with me." "That," said she, "depends upon me, not upon them." Concluding to ask for the best fare, that in her prices I might find a pretext for removing, I told her that I wished for a room in which I could be alone, a fire and light to burn throughout the night, my boots cleaned, and that I should not, on any account, be disturbed in the morning until I was ready to arise. I anticipated that she would charge so large a sum, that I should feel free to decline paying the amount, and thus honorably withdraw to seek more comfortable lodgings elsewhere. She named, however, the sum of one shilling, and, therefore, much to my disappointment, I felt under the necessity to remain for the night.

Being wearied and foot-sore with travelling for so long a distance under a pelting rain, I availed myself of these lodgings, poor as they were, even with thankfulness. Without supper, I retired, and enjoyed a sweet night's rest. Truly, the Lord can make us both to lie down and sleep in safety. I arose on the following morning with a strong desire for breakfast; but, to my surprise, everything appeared to be more unsettled than on the
6 *

night before. I therefore paid my bill and left my hostess, who, about a week after, sold out and removed to the United States. I mention the above as one of the experiences of a traveller.

From Bacup I went to Ashington, and thence to Sabden, to see a gentleman to whom I had been recommended by my friend Mr. Tucker, of Manchester. After walking about five miles in the rain, I arrived at his house in the twilight of the evening. Mr. Foster was absent. But when I had dried my clothing, I proceeded on my search about half a mile, and found him at his place of business, where I met with a gentleman standing outside. On approaching him, I inquired for Mr. Foster, when he announced that such was his name, and asked my business. I then presented a letter from Mr. Tucker, the handwriting of which he immediately recognized, and, requesting me to take his arm and receive shelter under his umbrella, we proceeded to his residence. After engaging in conversation and partaking of tea, we attended a prayer-meeting, where I was intro-duced to Mr. Foster's pastor, with whom I formed a very pleasant acquaintance. Notwithstanding my extreme fatigue, I addressed the meeting, with much satisfaction to my own soul, and, I trust, with profit to others. When the services were terminated, in company with the pastor, I returned to the residence of brother Foster, with whom we partook of supper, and engaged in prayer. We then conversed about Shiloh Baptist Church, for which Mr. Foster gave me twenty-five dollars, when, after gratefully receiving an invita·ion to remain for the night under his roof, and thus obviate the necessity of walking to Bacup in the thick rain and darkness, I gladly retired to rest.

In the morning, after commending ourselves to the Lord, and partaking of the bounties of His providence, Mr. Foster sent his servant, with a horse and gig, to take me to the railroad station. ten miles distant. I then pursued my way to Blackburn, Preston, and Hebdon Bridge (where I stayed two or three days), and other places in the neighborhood. From Hebdon Bridge I went to Salendine Nook, where I arrived on Saturday evening, after travelling on foot for nearly one-half of the day, in one of the wildest storms in the month of March. The exposure and fatigue to which I had been subjected caused a severe attack of dyspepsia, rendering me unfit for any labor until the afternoon of the following day.

Wearied and faint, I recommenced my work, and called on the Rev. John Stock, the pastor of the Baptist Church in Salendine Nook, whom I found residing in a very neat dwelling, known as "Patmos Cottage." Having informed him of the object of my visit, and requested a collection for its aid, he expressed some doubts whether my request could be granted, but kindly offered to introduce me to one of his deacons, that we might consult with him and decide upon a course of action. As I most willingly acceded to his proposition, we immediately started upon our walk to Bottom Hall, about half a mile distant. Upon being introduced to deacon Shaw, I was received not only with the affability of a true Christian gentleman, but also with the frankness and heartiness so peculiar to the people of Yorkshire. He invited me to take up my temporary abode in his house, promising me nothing, however, but food and lodging. After having engaged me to preach on the afternoon of the following day, should my health permit, and with the understanding that I was not to expect a collection, Mr. Stock returned to his home, leaving me under the hospitable roof of the excellent deacon. I found his family to consist of his wife and son—the latter appearing to

be a confirmed bachelor. Being comp.ete.y exhausted and overcome with fatigue, they employed
every available means to insure my comfort. The
son, whose room was very splendidly furnished,
insisted upon my using it, rather than run any
risk to my health by sleeping on a bed which had
not been occupied during the winter. This was
a favor which, I was informed by the deacon, was
quite unusual. As they conducted a very extensive business in woollen manufacture, they were
visited by gentlemen from all parts of the kingdom; but never before, as I was assured by the
father, had his son relinquished the occupancy of
his own room to a guest. Fully appreciating the
kindness, after supper and commending each other
to the care of our heavenly Father, I retired for
the night; but notwithstanding all the rich comforts by which I was surrounded, I enjoyed but
little rest. My almost sleepless night was followed
by the beautiful morning of the Sabbath. So
much was I suffering from pain, that I not only
doubted whether I should be able to preach in
the afternoon, but also feared that I was about to
have a severe sickness. Nevertheless, I determined to attend church and listen to Mr. Stock.

Mrs. Shaw, who was the deacon's second wife,

was a member of the Established Church, and reputed to be quite wealthy. Although the companion of an officer of the Baptist church, she had never accompanied her husband to public worship, and had never listened to the preaching of a Baptist minister. She was evidently unacquainted with the Faith, Principles, and Practices of the denomination; and, intimating that she regarded the Baptists as a very singular and prejudiced sect, asked me many questions concerning them. As Mrs. Shaw expressed a strong desire to hear me preach, notwithstanding that it was uncertain that I should be sufficiently recovered to fulfil my engagement, I recommended her to prepare herself and walk with us to the chapel, about half a mile distant. She remarked, however, that she had some hesitation in going, as, for more than two years that she had lived with the deacon, he had never once extended an invitation to her to accompany him. This information induced me to urge her very strongly to go in the afternoon, and thus surprise her husband. The deacon and myself then walked to the chapel, hoping to enjoy a delightful opportunity to sit together in a heavenly place—the place where God's honor delights to dwell.

Whilst on our way, deacon Shaw inquired of me what I was in the habit of preaching—whether I preached the Gospel or the Law—Jesus Christ or good works; "for," said he, "the people here live on the Gospel." Upon hearing my reply, he added, "Well, man, if you preach Christ to us, you may, perhaps, get a little something."

I have said that it was a pleasant morning; but three or four inches of snow (the largest quantity I saw in Europe at one time) covered the ground, and made the condition of the roads unfavorable to the assembling of a large congregation, especially as the majority of the attendants upon public worship must travel even to the distance of six or eight miles. Having, however, arrived at the chapel (a fine-looking and substantial building), and seeing the horses and vehicles which almost surrounded it, I was soon satisfied that there would be no lack of a congregation. I was soon introduced into the basement, where there were two large rooms, furnished with tables, chairs, &c. In one of them was placed a table, apparently about fifty feet long, covered with linen, plates, glass, cutlery, and all other things necessary, that the people might partake of a meal with comfort, the provision for which was brought

in their baskets. This I found to be an arrangement for dinner, to which friends were invited so
long as vacant seats remained, and made necessary by the long distance of the residence of
many of the worshippers, and the fact that there
was an intermission between the morning and
afternoon services of only one hour.

Another room, nearly equal in size to the one
already mentioned, was appropriated as a sitting
and smoking-room. There I saw a number of
ladies thus enjoying themselves after dinner—a
custom which I did not observe elsewhere in
England, although I doubt not that it was more
extensively observed.

At the time for morning service, we assembled
ourselves together, with others, in the chapel, and
listened to an interesting and deeply impressive
sermon, preached by the pastor, from the text
found in the Epistle to the Ephesians iii. 15—" Of
whom the whole family in heaven and earth are
named." At the close of the discourse, I was
announced to preach at one o'clock. The bene-
diction having been pronounced, most of the congregation adjourned to the basement—some to
eat, some to talk, and others to smoke. Being
introduced to many of the brethren, I briefly ex-

plained the nature of the object of my mission, and left them to discuss its merits.

The hour of the afternoon service having arrived, to the great surprise of her friends and all present, Mrs. Shaw was seen to enter the family pew. In fact, the circumstance was so unexpected by all, that it was difficult to determine whether my presence in the pulpit, or that of the deacon's wife in the pew, created the greatest sensation. I endeavored to preach from the prayer of Jabez— 1 Chron. iv. 10—"Oh, that thou wouldst bless me indeed!" Having unusual freedom, I could not but feel that, if ever I was sustained by the Holy Spirit in the delivery of my message, I most certainly was on that afternoon, in the Baptist Chapel, at Salendine Nook. After preaching, I stated to the audience that, as I had not been promised any collection, therefore I did not expect it, but I would retire to the basement, where I should be grateful to receive any donations for "Shiloh." Many of the congregation followed, some to extend Christian salutation, and invite me to visit their homes, and others to hand me their subscriptions. The pecuniary result of that afternoon's labor was altogether about one hundred dollars.

By special request, I preached again, in the

F 2

evening, about two miles distant from the chapel, being accompanied on foot to the place of meeting by the deacon and his family, including Mrs. Shaw. There we enjoyed another refreshing season. Upon our return, brother Shaw could not refrain expressing his delight that his wife had been attending Baptist church that day, and even iutimated that he regarded me as endowed with some extraordinary gift, remarking, at the same time, that he could not understand how it was that, whilst there had been many good preachers constantly coming to their church, which was one of the strongest in Yorkshire, his wife had never manifested the least disposition to hear one of them. "But with you," said he, "she is completely carried away." He then added, "I did not think that I should give you anything; but you have loosened my purse-strings; and, what is more, I have not known so much money to be contributed by our people for any object without previous notice.

During the week, I again preached to the same congregation, and received many cordial invitations to spend a few weeks with them; but, being anxious to prosecute my work to a close, the more especially as I was so much hindered in the commencement, I reluctantly declined the proffered kindness. Whilst, however, I remained, I used my utmost endeavors to counsel and instruct Mrs. Shaw, advising, her, also, to attend the same place of worship as her husband, and hear Mr. Stock, whenever it was convenient. This latter advice she promised to adopt.

As the time for my departure from a family and neighborhood where I had enjoyed many precious seasons, and received so much kindness, arrived, my dear friends expressed their regrets that we must part after so short an acquaintance. My preparations being made, my kind hostess presented me with a number of books and other articles, and a guinea for my private purse, enjoining upon me to remember her especially at the Throne of Grace. She earnestly invited me, also, to visit them again, and promised a comfortable home and a guinea for my own use whenever I could make it convenient to call upon them. I thought, at the time, that I might be able to see my friends once more before I left the country; but other engagements prevented me from enjoying so great a privilege. On the afternoon when I left, Mrs. Shaw conveyed me in her carriage, a distance of eight miles, to the railroad station, where I took leave of her, probably to see her no more in this world.

In the course of two or three weeks afterwards, I received a letter from brother Stock, in which he informed me of the baptism of Mrs. Shaw, and that she had connected herself with the Baptist church. He also expressed his kind regards towards me, his best wishes for my success, and the hope that the providence of God would once more permit me to visit Salendine Nook. I thought, truly, that God hath no respect to persons, and that, if I was faithful to Him, He would bless my labors amongst white as well as amongst colored persons. Surely, it is not by might nor by power, but the Spirit of the Lord, that this work is accomplished.

CHAPTER XVI.

HALIFAX—BRADFORD—LEEDS—IMPORTANT DOCUMENT—
HULL—SHEFFIELD—NOTTINGHAM—LEICESTER.

MY next trip was to Halifax, where I called on
the Rev. Mr. W——, who promised to lay the
case of the Shiloh Church before his deacons, and
invited me to preach for him on some evening
during the following week. To make the most of
my time, I visited Bradford, designing to return to
Halifax. Whilst there, I received a note from Mr.
W., informing me that it was deemed unadvisa-
ble for me to return, as the church made its own
collections, and then voted appropriations to the
different objects of Christian benevolence, so far
as their funds would allow. He closed with a
request for my address in London, that he might
forward me a donation; but I never again heard
from him.

My reception in Bradford was a true exemplifi-
cation of Christian courtesy. My cause was very
kindly commended by the faculty of Horton College (Rev. Dr. Acworth, President), where I was

invited to dine with the students as often as I would. I preached in both of the Baptist churches, and also lectured for the Independents at East Parade. At the latter place, a lady intimated to me her pleasure when seeing me enter the building, upon the occasion of a prayer-meeting, hoping that I was about to join the church, and her subsequent disappointment when she ascertained that her hopes were not to be realized. She desired that there should be at least one colored member in the church. I received from her a very liberal donation for the Shiloh Church.

My success in Bradford was much greater than I had anticipated, the amount collected being nearly three hundred dollars. Here, as elsewhere, I found many who were true friends; but all the time that I was in that country—I may say ever since I have been in the world—the Lord has never failed to raise up friends for me. He has ever been better to me than my fears or deserts. But in England I was especially led to contrast the difference of treatment which a colored man receives when travelling in that country and in America. Even Americans themselves seem not only to forget their wicked and foolish prejudices when in England, but appear to be ashamed to acknowledge that it ever existed in their minds. Upon the occasion of a public meeting, in which I had been invited and requested to speak, I met with a well-known doctor of divinity from the city of New York. When I addressed the meeting, I could not refrain from making the observation that, although the reverend gentleman and myself had often been together in religious meetings, that was the first time that I had ever met with him upon ministerial equality. Being inquired of if such was the fact, he immediately confessed its truthfulness and wickedness, and professed his determination to repent.

I recall with great pleasure the attention which I received from the faculty and students of the institutions of learning connected with the Baptist denominations in Bristol, Bradford, and London, and was gratified, most of all, by being assured of the fact that a promising young man of color, whose piety and talents were unquestionable, would be received into either of those colleges on equal terms with other students, upon my recommendation.

From Bradford I went to Leeds, where I found that the Baptists were building a chapel. This, it was thought, would be against my success.

But oelieving that my cause was the Lord's, and that the silver, and gold, and people are His, I determined not to be discouraged, but to prosecute diligently my master's business. Going forth in His strength, I was not disappointed. The Lord prospered my labors to that extent, that in Leeds and its immediate vicinity I collected about two hundred and fifty dollars.

I close this chapter with the insertion of the following address of the Baptists of Yorkshire to their brethren of the United States. It gives the sentiments not only of the churches by which it was immediately sent, but, in fact, of all the Christians of England:—

"DEAR BRETHREN:

"A colored brother and minister of Christ from amongst you, Mr. Jeremiah Asher, has visited us to solicit contributions towards discharging the debt on his chapel. Cordially responding to *your highly rezpectable* recommendation, and to the claims of his case, we have contributed, as we trust you will think, liberally towards it. We feel constrained, however, to embrace this opportunity of remonstrating with you, our brethren in Christ, on the strange inconsistency of the treatment which our and *your* colored brethren receive at your hands, and the strange difference between their treatment here in England, and in the free States of the Union. We have listened with interest to his preaching, and he has been gladly welcomed everywhere, both to our pulpits and to the firesides of every class of society. We think that you, brethren, must agree with us that we owe a debt to our colored brethren which it is not only our duty, but highly to our honor to discharge; and that in no way can we better discharge it than by showing to them our love as brethren in Christ, and by avoiding every word or deed, and even suppressing every feeling, which could make them *painfully* sensible of the grievous wrong which our progenitors have done to them.

"Brethren, we are confident that you must, as Christians, often feel that you bring no small guilt on your consciences in allowing yourselves to concur with the *children of this world* in keeping your most injured brethren in Christ at so great a social distance, and in so depressed a condition. If the *world* can, without compunction, refuse them equal social intercourse, and *practically* hold them down to SERVITUDE, though not in slavery, it must violate, brethren, *your* conscience and every Christian feeling, to do likewise.

"Brethren, we earnestly exhort you to break through these merely conventional yet sinful habits, and to honor your Master by your treatment of His servants. Be not ashamed of the brethren of Christ because the world is so, but let your light on this subject shine before men worthily of your profession. Happily, indeed, should we be to see our *Baptist* brethren *foremost* in America, not only in the emancipation of the colored people from personal slavery, but in the emancipation of *free men of color* from social degradation, in educating them and elevating them by every possible expedient; and foremost, too, in emanci-

7 G

pating themselves from a species of pride so irrational, so vulgar, and so *unchristian* as that of pride in difference of color.

"Although, brethren, you assign your liberality to *voluntary* emigrants from Europe as the cause of your inability to aid Mr. Asher's case, we must beg leave to remind you of two things: first, that colored men *now* in America are in the land of their *birth*, therefore in their *home*, and that 'charity should begin at home;' and next, that their *color* attests that they are the children of *compulsory* emigration, whose ancestors were dragged by *yours* from their fatherland, and that your fathers' heavy debt to *those* unhappy emigrants it is surely a sacred duty on your part to repay to their children.

"We trust, therefore, that our heartily expressed sympathy with Mr. Asher will not induce you to send to us other colored brethren on a similar errand. It would assuredly lead to disappointment. We hope, on the contrary, it will only stimulate you to contribute yourselves in aid of your colored *fellow-countryman's* spiritual wants, and also to elevate yourselves 'to the measure of the stature of the fulness of Christ,' by elevating these, His brethren and *your* brethren, to your own social standing."

Before bidding a final adieu to Yorkshire, I must refer to a singular circumstance which occurred during my short sojourn in Wakefield. A gentleman with whom I was well acquainted, and and who was formerly a member of the Church of England, having some misunderstanding with a

lady of the same church, was guilty of making
some disreputable statements concerning her. She
thereupon commenced legal proceedings against
him, and carried her case. As a part of his
penalty, he was compelled to walk the broad aisle
of the church in the presence of the whole congregation, with a sheet over his head, and then confess his wrong. This he was obliged to do by the
civil law, although he had long before left the
church, and united with the Baptists.

After collecting about fifty dollars in Mansfield,
I proceeded to Hull, the birthplace of William
Wilberforce, the slave's friend. I saw there the
splendid monument which had been erected to his
memory by the friends and advocates of freedom
in Great Britain. When I stood in the room in
which he was born, I felt that the place was holy
ground, especially when I recalled the burning
eloquence, the indefatigable labors, and untiring
zeal with which he ever advocated the cause of
the oppressed. I could not but silently lift my
heart in prayer to Almighty God, that He would
be pleased to raise up others to complete the work
that His servants, who now sleep in death, had
commenced, and, with unwavering love for the
bondman, had prosecuted.

I found the Baptist interest in Hull to be quite feeble. Although I spent but three or four days with the friends in that city, I preached for them, attended one or two social gatherings, and collected about thirty dollars.

As Hull was not only the birthplace, but the final resting-place of William Wilberforce, I found that his influence was strongly felt throughout the community. The people were thoroughly impregnated with the principle of liberty to the slave. Our sentiments, therefore, being in full accordance, I was received and treated by the citizens with the utmost cordiality.

From Hull, my journey extended to Sheffield, which is noted, the wide world over, for its extensive manufacturing of cutlery. The people of that city I found to be very kind and hospitable to strangers. By request, I preached in their chapels, and was made to feel quite at home, everything necessary being provided for my comfort. From both ministers and people, I did not receive in all England a warmer reception. God bless the people of Sheffield for what they did for little "Shiloh."! After staying there about ten days, I left for Nottingham, the residence of Rev. J. G. Pike, author of "Persuasives to Early Piety," and pastor of the Free-will Baptist Church. He received me most cordially, gave me a subscription, and invited me to preach in his chapel. My text upon that occasion was from John vi. 37— "Him that cometh to me I will in no wise cast out." I think that my discourse was rather too Calvinistic for the taste of the congregation, for they are not, by any means, admirers of John Calvin. There are two regular Baptist churches in the same place, one being under the pastoral care of the Rev. James Edwards, the other under that of the Rev. J. A. Baynes, who is esteemed to be one of the most popular men in Lancashire; but I found the churches to be comparatively weak interests. Both of the brethren united in aiding me, and I preached in both of their chapels. I collected in that city about forty dollars. Being anxious to visit as many other places as possible before leaving for home, I remained but a very short time, and then proceeded to Leicester, where the Rev. Robert Hall had spent the former part of his ministerial life. The present incumbent is the Rev. Mr. Mursell, whose talent and popularity are well known throughout the kingdom. Here, again, I was received with open hearts and doors, invited to take of the hospitalities of the people, and to preach in the Baptist pulpit. A family named Gould showed me especial kindness whilst I remained in the city. Mr. Gould gave me a considerable quantity of clothing for myself and family, as testimonials of his Christian regard for me.

Upon one afternoon, Mrs. Gould accompanied me to see a gentleman, with the view of soliciting a subscription. When we started, she expressed a desire to take my arm, saying that she could walk more comfortably. I apologized for not having previously extended that courtesy, on the plea that in my own country I was not . accustomed to walk on the streets with white ladies, and therefore was not forward to make the approach to her. She remarked that, in her case, no apology was necessary, as she regarded it as great an honor to walk with me as with any other gentleman. Arm in arm, we walked together through the streets of Leicester. Nor was this an isolated case of the same nature. In Manchester, Birmingham, London, and other places, I was received on equal terms with other gentlemen, irrespective of my complexion. I collected, in Leicester, about one hundred dollars.

CHAPTER XVII.

AFTER leaving Yorkshire, I went to Northampton to pay a visit to the Rev. J. T. Brown. Finding that he was out of town on my arrival, I took lodgings in a hotel in Bridge Street. On my journey thither from Hull, I lost a small bag, which, among other articles, contained a pair of steel-framed spectacles that I had been under the necessity of using almost constantly. I was obliged, therefore, to seek for another pair. Finding a jewelry-store, after a very little search, I entered to make my purchase. The business was conducted by two sisters. On seeing me, after other customers had been served, the eldest sister inquired whether I came from the East Indies. Telling her, in reply, whence I came, she expressed surprise, and remarked that she thought that the people were of a different complexion to mine. After enlightening her on this point, she asked if Americans generally spoke the English language.

151

I assured her that the English was my vernacular tongue, and knew no other. Then she proceeded to make many other inquiries as to the object of my visit, my profession, &c. I told her that I was a Baptist minister, and that my object was to raise means to assist the church of which I was pastor. She then offered to introduce me to Mr. Brown on the following day. When the younger sister entered the store, she was informed of the conversation which had transpired, and both agreed that, as I had engaged lodging only, to invite me to take all my meals with them, when not otherwise engaged, which invitation I very gladly accepted, providing that Mr. Brown should not make different arrangements.

On the following morning, one of the ladies conducted me to see the Baptist minister, remarking, on the way, that she imagined that Mr. Brown would be surprised to see her, as she did not attend his meeting, being a Methodist, although her father, for many years previous to his death, was a deacon, and her mother a prominent working-member of the Baptist church. Having arrived at Mr. Brown's residence, I sent him my letter of introduction, which speedily brought him to welcome us in person. My lady friend excused herself for

calling on Saturday, with the plea that she was
desirous of ascertaining whether I should preach
on the Sabbath. After expressing his pleasure
in seeing her, Mr. Brown requested her to make
known among her friends that I would preach in
his chapel on the following afternoon. Then,
wishing to be kindly remembered to her sister,
who was an attendant on his ministry, they separated.

After her departure, Mr. Brown inquired in
what way I became acquainted with the family.
When I related the circumstances, he regarded
them as being quite providential. He then gave
me some account of the family history. Their
parents were wealthy, and had been among the
most liberal supporters of the cause of Christ,
both at home and abroad. Since their decease,
the elder sister had become connected with the
Methodist church; while the younger, who was
esteemed to be one of the most amiable and accomplished ladies in Northampton, continued to
attend the Baptist chapel. Notwithstanding their
wealth, he regarded it as almost impossible to
obtain a subscription from them for any purpose;
and, while he persuaded me to urge my claim
very strongly, suggested that, in case of success, I

7 *

would be the first man who had received a subscription in that house since the death of the
father.

We then made our arrangements for the following day.   On the Sabbath morning, as agreed, I
attended service at the Baptist chapel, and listened
to a very impressive discourse on "The Meekness
of Christ," from Rev. Mr. Brown.   I preached in
the same place in the afternoon, and took a collection.   In the evening, I preached in the house
once occupied by the renowned Dr. Doddridge.
To me, it was a delightful day.   I enjoyed some
degree of liberty at both services, and felt it to be
a great honor to stand where men of world-wide
renown had before preached Jesus Christ to poor
sinners.

On Monday morning, I again called on my
friends, and, soliciting a donation, received from
them ten dollars, with a renewed offer of my hospitality during my sojourn in the city.   Mr.
Brown congratulated me upon my success, and
expressed the opinion that, after that, I need not
despair of succeeding anywhere.   Observing that
Miss Martha, the younger of the two sisters, was
apparently quite thoughtful on the subject of
religion, I availed myself of every convenient

opportunity to converse and pray with her, trusting in the Lord to accompany with His blessing, the word spoken. Many an hour have I spent with Miss Martha in endeavoring to persuade her to repent. She was most amiable in her deportment, and in every respect the lady; yet one thing she lacked.

My stay in Northampton was one of the most agreeable which I had known in England, although it only lasted one week, being necessarily thus brief, as I was about bringing my labors in that country to a termination. I left with great reluctance, feeling that, if I could stay, the Lord would give me souls for my hire. A few weeks after my leaving, I received a note from Mr. Brown, saying that the Lord had been pleased to make me the instrument of Miss Martha's conversion. That was soon followed by a letter from the sister herself, giving an account of her conversion, baptism, and love to the Saviour, also expressing her warmest gratitude for the interest which I had manifested in her spiritual welfare. That was one of the most encouraging epistles I ever received. Shortly after, and just before my leaving the country, I received another letter from the same hand, full of encouragement to me to persevere in the great and glorious work of preaching Christ to poor sinners. Surely the Lord has been good and gracious in blessing my feeble efforts, for I know that my labors have not been in vain. For this and all success, I desire to humble myself as I acknowledge His mighty power, and to be un-feignedly thankful.

My arrival in the city of London occurred about the 20th of April, 1850. My ears were very speedily greeted with the mournful intelli-gence of the decease of my good brother, Mark Moore, who had for a long time the reputation of keeping a good Baptist tavern in the great metro-polis of the world. This made the second of my landlords who had been removed by the hand of death during my short stay in the country, and both by that awful scourge—cholera. This latter brother was taken with the disease on the day that I left London on my previous visit for Bir-mingham. On the evening of that day, he was a corpse. The Rev. C. M. Birrell, of Liverpool, gave me a kind letter of introduction to Mr. Moore, stating my object, and expressing the hope that I should be cordially treated. I was, there-fore, very kindly entertained for about ten dollars a week—a very reasonable sum for board and lodging in London. I here ascertained that the Rev. Dr. Cushman, whose polished eloquence is so well known in this country, had married their daughter.

Upon my first visit to London, my pecuniary means were almost entirely exhausted. Feeling, therefore, that I must prosecute my work with the greatest diligence, I called upon Mr. John Haddon, the well-known Baptist printer, and a member of the Rev. John Howard Hinton's church. After a full examination of my documents, he expressed the opinion that the case, however deserving and truthful it might be, had no strong claim upon British Christians; furthermore, that the money ought to be raised in Philadelphia, and that American churches were far more able than the English to assist their colered brethren. He very kindly agreed, however, to publish some circulars, at an expense of fifteen dollars, and wait for the payment until I had succeeded in raising the amount. He then sent me to B. W. Gurney, Esq., who contributed ten dollars. That was the first donation which I received in England; and I cannot but believe that the influence of his name, not only in London, but throughout England, had very much to do with my subsequent success.

Calling upon Mr. Haddon a short time after my return, on my second visit to London, I was enabled to show him my subscription-book, when he expressed his surprise and pleasure at the amount collected. Having next paid his bill for printing, he greatly assisted me by his advice as to the best way to proceed in London, which advice I thankfully received and adopted; and, whenever he met me afterwards, he manifested a degree of interest for my success, and always treated me with Christian consideration.

CHAPTER XVIII.

WHEN in Rochdale, Yorkshire, and enjoying
the hospitalities of Mr. Kellsall, he gave me a letter of introduction to Samuel Peto, Esq., a member of Parliament for London, whom he mentioned
to me as being his son-in-law. Mr. Peto enjoys
the reputation of being one of the most wealthy
and liberal men in the metropolis. I was informed
that he erected, at his own cost, the most beautiful Baptist edifice in Bloomsbury, London, occupied by the Rev. Dr. Brock, of whose church he
was an active member. Upon presenting my
letter, Mr. Peto invited me to take breakfast with
him the following morning, when he gave me
twenty dollars, and always afterwards, when we

met, treated me with Christian kindness and consideration.

As it was necessary to my success that I should obtain recommendations from leading Baptist ministers and others, I made an early call, one morning, on the Rev. Wm. Brock, with my certificates again in hand. After I had taken breakfast with him, and led in family devotions, he carefully examined into the whole matter, gave me a sovereign and the following recommendation :—

" Few cases have stronger claims on our Christian liberality than the one herewith presented by my friend, Mr. Asher. The merits of the case are singularly strong, and the character of Mr. Asher such as must commend his application to the generous attention of the churches of Christ. WILLIAM BROCK,
Bloomsbury Chapel.

Among the many who gave me strong testimonials whilst in London, I have in my possession those signed by the Hon. and Rev. Baptist W. Noel, the Rev. Drs. Cox, Hoby, Burns, Steane, Overbury, with the Rev. Messrs. F. Trestrail, John Aldis, James Smith, B. Lewis, Joshua Russell, of Blackheath, and George Thompson, Esq., M. P. The latter I publish for obvious reasons :—

"WATERLOO PLACE, *May* 28, 1850.

"I have this day enjoyed the privilege of a lengthened interview with Mr. Asher, and have been inspired with a deep interest in the success of the object which has brought him to this country. The foregoing pages show that he has not appealed in vain to those who profess a regard for the improvement of the social, moral, and religious condition of the colored people of the United States. I trust he will experience little difficulty in raising the amount still necessary to liquidate the debt which presses at present very heavily upon the people to whose spiritual good he has devoted himself. A contribution given to Mr. Asher will not only be an act of generosity towards a struggling society, but a practical testimony against a cruel prejudice which has hitherto depressed and proscribed a large class of the population of America. I most cordially add my humble recommendation to the many which this book contains from men eminent for their piety and philanthropy.

GEORGE THOMPSON.

The larger part of my subscriptions in London was obtained by direct and personal application. I remained there about two months, which gave me ample time and opportunity to see almost every part of that world-renowned city. I found the facilities for travelling such that I could ride the entire length or breadth of the city for sixpence, or twelve cents; and in all my travelling in Great Britain I was never once refused a seat in a public conveyance. But in Philadelphia no

G 2

colored persons, except almost white, are allowed a right enjoyed by the lowest dregs of society, if only white, thus encouraging deception and hypocrisy, and practically offering a reward to amalgamation, if not to licentiousness.

My time, however, would not allow me to visit specially any public places of interest, but such as fell immediately in my way. Among these was the Tower of London, through nearly the whole of which I was taken by the porters having charge of the Tower. There I saw the cell of Sir Walter Raleigh, on the walls of which was engraven his name by his own hand; the gate from which Queen Mary departed to the executioner's block; the variety of armor worn by the British officers and soldiery of different reigns; the different styles of deadly weapons used on the field of conflict; and, last of all, the crowns and sceptres, with other paraphernalia, used at the coronation of the different sovereigns of Britain from the time of William the Conqueror downwards. Such sights worked their natural effect upon a republican mind, and I turned away only to rejoice in the simplicity of the form of government practically adopted in my own country, notwithstanding that I might think that she seems to have forgotten its true spirit and design.

I was honored, whilst in this city, in being permitted to preach in at least three of the chapels, and to address two or three Sabbath-schools. I was also privileged to attend several anniversary meetings in the month of May, when I met with brethren from several parts of the kingdom, whom it had been my privilege to see before, and held kindly intercourse with them. In all of those meetings, without exception, I was treated with the utmost consideration, and urged to take some part in the exercises. The brethren made me to forget, for a time, that I was ever, in any place, disfranchised on account of my color. Those meetings were seasons among my best recollections of the past, and my best expectations for the future. There was nothing, either by word, look, or deed, which was designed or calculated to remind me of the superiority of my white brethren to myself; but, on the other hand, they said that they felt and rejoiced that we were all "one in Christ Jesus." In fine, this was my treatment throughout all England. I travelled nearly over the entire realm, was entertained most hospitably in many of the first families, as my testimonials and diary will show; but never in a single instance, either publicly or privately, was I reminded in any way of my difference of race, excepting in the case of the *friend*, referred to elsewhere, who had professed strong friendship for the colored man, and deep sympathy with an unfortunate and oppressed people.

Whilst I am knowingly digressing from my main point, I cannot refrain from mentioning those circumstances which formed so striking a contrast in the treatment received by the colored man in the two countries. I venture to assert that no man possessed of the same sensitive temperament as myself can meet with his white brethren in America without occasionally having his equilibrium disturbed, all his religion to the contrary notwithstanding; for they are bound to insult him, either by treating him with silent contempt, or saying something which they know, and he knows, and God knows is calculated to make him feel that his company is unwelcome. For my own part, I have long since understood this, and have acted accordingly. On the other hand, a colored Christian cannot stay for any length of time in England without being made to realize that his treatment, like the Sabbath, is a season of rest, and an earnest of good things to come, which may God hasten in His own good time!

My collections in London were of a smaller amount than in many other places in England, owing partly to the fact that the more wealthy portion of the Christian citizens resided in the suburbs, and were therefore difficult to approach, and partly to the uncertainty of reaching them in their city offices. But yet I cannot close my remarks upon London without special reference to my friend, deacon Samuel Gale, barrister-at-law, living No. 70 Bazinghall Street, who was baptized by the Rev. Dr. Rippon, and who, if still living, undoubtedly holds the office of deacon in Rev. Mr. Spurgeon's church. He manifested towards me much kindness, as he had formerly done towards the late Rev. Thomas Paul, of Boston, whose accounts to a very considerable amount Mr. Gale informed me that he had audited. By the following certificate, it will be seen that he examined my accounts so far as the 20th of September, 1850, including the amount which had been realized and paid over by bills of exchange to Rev. B. R. Loxley.

After going through the whole book, he declared:—

" Examined and found correct."
.SAMUEL GALE,
70 *Bazinghall Street, London.*"

In addition to the above, I present the following :—

" We beg to state that the utmost reliance may be placed
in the accuracy of Mr. Gale's examination of the foregoing
accounts; and, further, that, in our opinion, Mr. Asher's
expenses have been surprisingly small, viz., £143, 17*s.*, 10*d.*,
and we rejoice that so large a sum as £525 have been secured, clear of all expenses, for the object.
FRED. TRESTRAILL,
Sec'y Baptist Missionary Society.
JAMES HOBY, D. D.
WILLIAM GROSER,
JOSEPH ANGUS, L.L. D."

In addition:—

" I have long had the pleasure of knowing Mr. Gale, and
cheerfully testify to his high professional respectability.
EDWARD STEANE, D. D."

Having so far accomplished my work in London, I left many kind friends to see them no more
until we meet above. My landlady and her entire
household deserve my lasting gratitude for the
many kindnesses shown me; and my prayer is
that the blessing of Him who has graciously pro.
mised to be a Husband to the widow, and a

Father to the fatherless, may ever rest upon them! "I was a stranger, and they took me in."

During the latter part of my mission to London, I occupied lodgings in Gravesend, a seaport thirty miles distant, which I found to be a very beautiful place, and quite a resort for Londoners during the warm weather. I preached in Zion Chapel, of that town, addressed the Sunday-school, and also received a contribution for my object.

My visit to Gravesend concluded my tour in England, throughout nearly the whole of which I had been permitted to travel. In every city and village I was received hospitably, and treated with Christian affection, and recognized by every child of God as a man and a brother. My impressions of the whole country were mainly those of surprise and wonder, especially during my visit in London. Notwithstanding all that I had heard and read of the great metropolis, when I saw it I could not but be reminded of the words of the Queen of Sheba to Solomon, that "the half had not been told" me. So ended my journeyings in England.

When my work was done in that city, being anxious to see Edinburgh, if but one day, I took my departure for Scotland. I was daily expecting to hear from a friend who had engaged to procure me a passage for the United States. I remained in the city of palaces about a week, but made few acquaintances, excepting with those immediately connected with the Baptist churches. One of the churches had three pastors, from the presiding one of which I received the following testimonial:—

"EDINBURGH, *Sept.* 29, 1860.

"The Baptist church in Bristo Street received Mr. Jeremiah Asher, as a brother beloved in the Lord, to communion in the ordinance of the Lord's Supper and the other ordinances of social worship. Mr. Asher preached a most impressive and Scriptural discourse, by which the brethren were much refreshed and edified. They cordially and affectionately send their Christian salutations to the dear brethren and sisters over whom the Holy Spirit hath made him an overseer, and commend him to God and the Word of His grace.

"In the name of the church   H. H. DICKIE,
One of the Pastors.

I also received the following from the Elder Street Church:—

EDINBURGH, *Sept.* 30., 1850.

"I have great pleasure in recommending the case of Mr. Asher and his church in Philadelphia to the consideration of fellow Christians. Mr. Asher has both addressed a meeting and preached a sermon in Elder Street Church, much to the satisfaction of those who heard him. His doctrine is

sound and truly Scriptural, his manner earnest, and his spirit
throughout that of a man who has felt the power of the
grace of God in his own soul. May the great God our
Saviour send him back to his flock with an abundant blessing !   J. WATSON,
                    Minister, Elder Street Church."

Here I protracted my stay for two or three
days, more to see the city and its curiosities, than
from any expectation or inducement which I had
that I should receive pecuniary assistance. I
visited Sir Walter Scott's monument, the Castle,
and other places of interest. I then went to Glasgow, there to close my labors, and then to bid
adieu to the many and interesting friends whom I
had made in Great Britain in the space of about
fourteen months.

A few days in Glasgow will close up my account of what I saw and felt in that land of
liberty. Glasgow, though the last city visited, is
not by any means the least in my esteem. During
my stay there, I received all that was necessary
to cause me to feel that I was welcome to the
hearts, houses, and churches of the people. I
preached once, and addressed two or three other
meetings. The Baptists in Glasgow are not numerous. Among other kind friends in that city,
I met with the late Robert Kettle, Esq., of whose
8 H

decease I have been lately informed by the Rev.
Mr. Girdwood, of New Bedford, Mass. Mr. Kettle
was esteemed as one of the most kind, humane,
and liberal-hearted men in all Scotland. At the
time of his death, as a testimonial of their appreciation of his worth, the citizens of Glasgow
assembled *en masse* to attend his funeral. He certainly had been a very hospitable and philan-
thropic man, kind to strangers, and careful to
entertain them, not knowing but that thereby he
might be entertaining angels unawares.

My visit to Glasgow closed up one of the most
delightful, and, I doubt not, one of the most successful years of my life, inasmuch as I feel that it
must be profitable to me in my future labors and
conflicts in the cause of my Master. The remembrance of my association with some of the best
men in the world, of listening to their counsel,
remarking their examples, of learning the intense
interest which British Christians, and philanthropists generally, entertain regarding the elevation
of our down-trodden race—being made conscious
of their strong desire to break off the yoke, and
let the oppressed go free—surely such lessons I
ought not to forget. Neither can I fail to remem-

ber the favor and the uniform kindness, the warm
affection and Christian courtesy, manifested to me
in every town and hamlet which I visited in that
vast empire. It is, therefore, my prayer that the
rich blessing of God may ever rest upon them
all! Amen.

> Kind friends, I bid you all adieu!
> Homeward I turn my wishful eye;
> If not again on earth we meet,
> A grateful heart bids all good-bye!
> When all our work on earth is done,
> May we in heaven through Christ be one!

CHAPTER XIX.

RETURN VOYAGE—RECEPTION ON BOARD THE STEAMER "CITY OF GLASGOW"—A PROSPEROUS VOYAGE, AND SAFE RETURN HOME.

MY mission being completed in England, so far as it was practicable, I took passage in the steamer "City of Glasgow" (Captain Matthews), bound for New York, in October, 1850. As all the berths in the second cabin had been previously engaged, I was compelled to take one in the first cabin—a privilege with which very few colored persons have been favored on board the ocean steamers. My berth was midship; therefore my seat was at the centre of the table. We left Glasgow at 12 o'clock, M., on Saturday, were towed down the Clyde as far as Greenock, and went to sea on Sunday, about 3 o'clock, P. M.

When my passage was engaged, inquiries were made of the captain whether the fact of my being a colored man would subject me to different treatment from the other passengers. To these, he replied that, if I paid the same fare, I should

172

receive, in all respects, the same privileges. Being then introduced to him as a Baptist clergyman, he promised to see that every provision should be made for my comfort. There were on board five or six other ministers, of different denominations, among them the Rev. Dr. Kennedy, with his wife, of Troy, N. Y. It so happened that his seat at the table was next to mine. There was also a gentleman from New Orleans, accompanied by his wife and another lady, whose seats were directly opposite. When they came to dinner on the first day, this *gentleman* appeared to be much excited, and sending, in his anger, for the captain, inquired of him if he allowed "niggers" at his table. Capt. M. replied in the negative. "Well," said the gentleman, pointing at me, "there is one." The captain then remarked: "That is Mr. Asher, from America, who has been introduced to me as a gentleman, and a clergyman of the Baptist denomination. I have received the same amount of passage money from him as from you, and cannot, therefore, interfere. But if you object to sit at the same table with him, other arrangements shall be made for you equally as good." Thus the controversy ended. He took his seat, but for a day or two appeared to be quite uneasy. Soon, however, he apparently became quite reconciled; and, for the remainder of the voyage, no one was treated by him and others with more politeness and consideration than myself.

The gentlemanly bearing of the captain made things pleasant and agreeable for the rest of the voyage. There were two reverend gentlemen, whose names I will not mention (for I have reason to believe they have repented), who at first showed some symptoms of being *troubled* at my presence; but, hearing the answer of the captain to the Southern gentleman, and seeing the kind attention shown me by him, they also became very attentive to me; an old acquaintance was renewed. One of these I remembered when he was a charity scholar in Brown University. He was then pastor of a country church in Connecticut. My aunt was a member of his church. He sat by me, and turned his back upon me. He and his wife were talking French; and it seemed as if it was with difficulty that either could speak a word of English. After he found that I knew him, he apologized, and spoke in English. Both of these gentlemen treated me with kind attention afterwards, and told me, if ever I came to their places,

I would be welcome to a seat at their tables, and beds in their houses.

One of these I have since visited for the purpose of ascertaining whether his repentance was sincere, and I have every reason to believe he was converted. So it should be in all of the public conveyances where colored persons are proscribed. If the proprietors were men of principle, and firm for the right, they would have no trouble about settling the question in favor of their own interest.

On the Sabbath morning, during breakfast, the captain informed us that it was his custom to hold religious services on the Lord's day, and that, when there was no clergyman on board, he was accustomed to read the service of the Episcopal church; but as he was now favored with so many preachers, he would appoint a committee to make arrangements for three services, to be held on each Lord's day during the voyage. He named me as chairman of this committee. He stated that it would be desirable, as so large a number of passengers was on board, to hold services in the first and second cabins at the same hour. The committee having retired to make arrangements for the day, it was strongly urged upon me that I should fill the first appointment.

To this I objected, on the plea that the doctors of divinity should have the pre-eminence. Finally, Dr. Kennedy was appointed to preach in the first cabin, and three others to make the arrangements for the day. I was selected to preach in the evening. Thus six services were provided for. At all of these services, the preachers were listened to with much attention and profit. By the time of the commencement of the evening service, we were visited with a most terrible storm. The sea had become so rough, that it was almost impossible to stand. Nevertheless, I attempted to preach, although, whilst delivering my discourse, I was under the necessity of clinging to the table. The text which I used on that dreadful night may be found in the 57th Psalm and 1st verse—"Be merciful unto me, O God, be merciful unto me; for my soul trusteth in thee: yea, in the shadow of thy wings will I make my refuge, until these calamities be overpast."

The "City of Glasgow" was supposed to be in danger of being lost that night; and indeed it was an awful night, such an one as I hope never to see again. Upon the subsidence of the storm, we went into the port of Belfast, after being out twenty-four hours, to take in an additional supply of coal. We were again soon on our way, and arrived safely in New York, after a passage of seventeen days, fully appreciating the kind attention which we had received from the gentlemanly officers. There we parted, some to meet no more until summoned by the great Archangel to stand before the Judgment Seat.

I went immediately to pay a visit to my family, who still resided in Providence. We rejoiced together in the Lord that He had kept us all in safety, prospered me in my labors, and improved me in bodily health, thus strengthening me for His service for the future, and laying me under lasting gratitude for the blessings of His providence.

8 *

CHAPTER XX.

HAVING spent two or three weeks in Providence, I left for Philadelphia, where I received
a most cordial welcome from the members of the
Shiloh Baptist Church.   But I found, much to
my surprise and sorrow, that a sad change had
taken place.   Some, whom I had regarded as
pillars of the church, had left for other places;
others had gone to join the church above; so
that, notwithstanding my success in England, I
had great heaviness of heart; but, still determined
to be of good courage, and to trust in the Lord, I
resolved to enter diligently upon my labors, and
restore, so far as possible, that which was lost.

Very soon after my return to Philadelphia, a
large meeting was held in the Shiloh Baptist

Church to receive my report. The Rev. Howard Malcom, D. D., was chosen to preside; and the Rev. J. Newton Brown was appointed Secretary. The report was read, and enthusiastically received. A series of resolutions was then offered and adopted, expressive of the approbation of the church of the entire course pursued by the pastor in his representation of the church in England, and of their gratitude to the friends of the oppressed for the kind reception given him, and the substantial aid afforded; also extending the thanks of the church to the pastor for his promptness in remitting his collections to Rev. B. R. Loxley, the Treasurer of the Building Fund. It was then ordered that the doings of the meeting be published in three of the papers of the denomination. I could not refrain from congratulating the church and congregation upon their success, and the almost immediate prospect of being relieved from the pressure of a heavy debt, as we had now reduced our mortgage to two thousand dollars. A proposition was then made by some of the brethren to make a further reduction, by an immediate subscription. About two hundred were subscribed during the meeting, but not one-half of the sum was ever collected.

The pecuniary affairs of the church rested here for about four years, when, thinking that we were quite safe, I determined to give my whole attention to its spiritual condition. Accordingly, we gave ourselves unto prayer, to seek the quickening power and converting grace of God. But for an entire year, there was not in our midst, so far as I know, one conversion to God. From 1850 to 1854, we received into the church seven members by baptism, and nineteen by letter, experience, &c. That was the most dreary season I have experienced during all my connection with the church.

At that stage of our history, we had to contend with some opposition from the other colored churches of the city. They being, apparently, in a prosperous condition, the large number of persons who came to the city with letters of dismission were induced to join their ranks. Strangers were informed of the precarious condition of the Shiloh Church—that we were in debt, and that the house was likely to be sold. Whilst, however, the fact of this opposition was a great obstacle to our progress, we determined still to trust and to labor.

We continued to maintain all our regular meetings, which, considering the small number of our

membership, were invariably well attended. At
length, in gracious answer to our prayers, the
Lord was pleased to pour down upon us His
Holy Spirit; and for some time souls were daily
converted to Christ. For months in succession,
we enjoyed the privilege of disturbing the bap-
tismal waters. During this revival, we held no
extra services; our congregation increased; the
membership of the church was much encouraged
and strengthened, and the confidence of the public was secured. The meetings were all free from
animal excitement, and of the most delightful
character. And now, as we look back upon those
days of spiritual enjoyment, when the Holy Spirit
was manifestly in our midst, we are inclined to
sing with the poet:—

"Once, O Lord, thy garden flourished;
  Every plant was gay and green;
  Then thy Word our spirits nourished—
  Happy seasons we have seen."

On the third Sabbath in March, 1855, it was
my privilege to baptize four happy converts, and
to receive into the church one by letter. The
third Sabbath in April, when nine converts were
baptized, and one was received by letter, was a

day long to be remembered. Among those baptized, was my own dear daughter, aged between seventeen and eighteen years. She had been a child of much anxious solicitude and many prayers. Her conversion and baptism were occasions of gratitude and joy to a father's heart, enhanced by my being permitted to administer the ordinance. Hail and snow made the day one of the most unpleasant of the season; yet, notwithstanding this, one of the largest congregations ever convened in the Meeting-house, assembled both morning and afternoon. At the hour of the administration of the Lord's Supper, the house was filled to its utmost capacity.

The third Sabbath in May was another bright day in our church calendar. Surely, the rod of His strength went forth from Zion. We received ten by baptism (eight of whom were baptized in the house, and two in the Schuylkill), and ten by letter, being the largest number ever received into the church at one time. "Then said they among the heathen, The Lord hath done great things for them. Truly, the Lord hath done great things for us, whereof we are glad."

On the third Lord's day in June, three persons were added by baptism, and two by letter. In

July, two were received by letter. In September, two were added by baptism, and one by letter. Thus it appears that six months out of seven, the waters were troubled, whilst no extra meetings were held, nor was foreign aid employed. Our faith was in God, and in the power of His might. We used the means, and He blessed our labors. We were constrained to acknowledge that the work was His; and while we preached, and prayed, and labored to the best of our ability, we gave Him all the praise and all the glory. It was God who killed and made alive again. Looking back from this distant stand-point of time, and reflecting upon the labors and faith of the church, I regard it as one of the most precious seasons of revival I ever enjoyed. It certainly greatly strengthened us, for never was the church more united or happy than at that time. May the Lord, from the rich abundance of His grace, grant many more such seasons unto Shiloh!

Soon after this, our attention was directed to our remaining indebtedness on the building, the balance of the money remaining on mortgage being demanded. Upon full investigation, we ascertained our whole debt to amount to thirty-two hundred dollars. I was again disheartened and ready to halt. To raise so large a sum of money within a given time, appeared to me to be a moral impossibility. To go abroad again to collect money for the same object as before was was out of the question. I therefore resolved to call an advisory council of the pastors and dea-cons of some of the Baptist churches in Philadel-phia. Yet, notwithstanding this resolution, I felt that the end had come; we should lose our beau-tiful house; our hope would be destroyed, and the prophecies of our enemies fulfilled.

When the council met, the whole subject was laid before them, and, as might be expected, there was found to be much difference of opinion. Some of the brethren argued in favor of abandoning the interest; whilst others argued that it should be continued, if I would give myself to the col-lection of the money within twelve months. They also generously proposed to supply my pulpit during that time. After prayerful deliberation and consultation with my friends, I acceded to the proposition, provided that the whole sum could be raised in Philadelphia, and that all the brethren present would aid me to the utmost of their ability. To all this they agreed. Deacon

John C. Davis, of the First Church, took the first effective step towards raising the amount, by contributing fifty dollars. Other members of the council agreed to raise one hundred dollars each, provided that the whole amount needed was subscribed within one year. I subscribed to this debt one hundred dollars. Then followed deacon Frank Williams, of the Shiloh Church, with a subscription of one hundred dollars.

About this time, the Lord sent us help by the unwearied and efficient labors of the Rev. Thomas S. Malcom, for whose services the Shiloh Church is laid under lasting obligation. He agreed to collect, upon the condition above stated, three hundred dollars. That pledge he more than redeemed; whilst, in every way possible, he aided us both temporally and spiritually. His labors were highly acceptable to the church, and blessed by the Lord. Through his instrumentality, we established a Monday Evening Prayer-Meeting, to pray for two specific objects, viz., a Revival of religion, and pecuniary assistance.

The mortgage was held by a member of the church, who professed to be much embarrassed for the want of funds. As an extra inducement

H 2

to diligence, he offered that, if I would raise in
some way the amount of the mortgage, he would
subscribe one hundred dollars, and he would
allow me the use of the interest due him, which
then amounted to about five hundred dollars, ,
as long as I continued with Shiloh Church, without interest, as a token of his regard and appreciation of service rendered to the church. This
was an act of benevolence which he did not wish
to be made public. My first effort was to raise
the money to relieve him, in which I soon succeeded without much difficulty. We agreed that
he should receive the whole amount, transfer the
mortgage, pay his subscription, and then fulfil his
promise to me. In addition to the above, I had
collected one hundred and sixty dollars on the
interest. This being done, previous to raising
the amount on the mortgage, he permitted me to
use the sum, on my giving a note, until such a
time as the whole arrangement should be completed. He soon received the money, and, within
a short time after, lost it, and rumor says con-
siderably more, in some of the gambling places
of this city. Only one dollar of his subscription
was ever paid. Nothing was done towards re-

deeming his pledge to me. My note was sold, and I was compelled to pay the one hundred and sixty dollars, with interest and costs of prosecution. It is almost needless to add that he was excluded from the church, and his career in Philadelphia ended.

CHAPTER XXI.

MY work was now to pursue vigorously the task of collecting subscriptions. Taking advantage of my experience in England, and knowing that I should meet with many discouragements, as well as many things to cheer me, I girded myself for the effort, determined not to go out of the city of Philadelphia. My first applications were made to the wealthy men of the city, many of whom assisted me with much liberality. I gave myself to the work five or six days in every week, and reported the subscriptions from time to time in the *Christian Chronicle*, that I might keep the object constantly before the public. One application which I made to a member of the Spruce Street Church afforded me, at a time when I most needed it, so much encouragement, that I cannot refrain from mentioning the circumstance. Although well acquainted with all the difficulties of

188

collecting, I had not succeeded so rapidly as I thought I ought to have done, and was becoming disheartened. Cast down and perplexed, I went to the place of business of the brother alluded to above; but I could scarcely state my case intelligently. He seemed to anticipate the difficulty, talked kindly to me, and, giving me a check for fifty dollars, wished me success in my undertaking, and prosperity in the church.

When in England on the same mission, I was recommended to call upon a wealthy gentleman who resided in Birmingham. He received me with courtesy, listened attentively to my story, and then, giving me ten dollars, thanked me for calling upon him, remarking, at the same time, that he was always glad to assist a minister of the Lord Jesus Christ, whether he wore a gown or not. I received many donations of a like sum in England, but never one that gave me so much encouragement. "The Lord loveth the cheerful giver." There are those who often give liberally, yet do so in such a way as to confer but little benefit. When brethren design to give, they should do it cheerfully, that they may encourage the heart and strengthen the hands of him who may be called to that peculiar department of

Christian labor. Then will the work be much more speedily accomplished, and with less expense, besides saving the injuring of the feelings of those who ask for the Lord's money. A gift bestowed in such a spirit will be "twice blessed— blessing him that gives and him that takes."

I will illustrate my meaning by giving an anecdote in contrast with the above. Whilst making collections in England, the Rev. Mr. Haycroft, pastor of the Broadmead Church, whose munificent kindness I have already mentioned, desired that I should call upon a gentleman who had the reputation of being one of the most benevolent men in the city. Mr. Haycroft took especial pains to introduce me, and make him acquainted with the object of my mission. Having sent him one of my circulars, fully setting forth the particulars, I called upon him at his place of business. Immediately that he saw me, he arose from his seat, laid his hand upon me, and showed me the door, telling me never to come there again. I was overpowered with surprise; but, on returning to my room, I determined to write the gentleman a note. In that, I said that had I not supposed him to be a gentleman and a Christian, I should not have called upon him, and very much regretted to have found myself mistaken. I acknowledged that I had no right to dictate as to the appropriation of his money ; but I did dispute his right to insult and maltreat me, and I could not believe that any true gentleman would be guilty of such contemptible conduct. He sent me a guinea without replying to my note. True, there were five dollars, but with a very large discount of the blessing. Should any who read these pages have any of the Lord's money when His stewards call for it, let me earnestly recommend them to bestow it cheerfully, that a blessing may rest upon them.

But to return from this digression. Having effected all that was possible by personal application, receiving subscriptions ranging from ten to one hundred dollars, I made a request of several churches to aid us by a contribution of one hundred dollars each, and that I should be permitted to make an individual appeal until that sum was realized. To this arrangement, the First, Second, Tenth, Twelfth, and Spruce Street Churches consented. From two of them, however, I did not collect more than half of the sum mentioned.

Our own little Shiloh took hold of the work with a commendable zeal. More than seven hun-

dred dollars were paid by my own congregation.
"The people had a mind to work" and to give.
Brother Frank Williams, and others of our brethren and sisters, not only gave freely of their means,
but strengthened my hands and encouraged my
heart. Of brother Williams, it may be said that
he was doing his last work. Before the object in
view was accomplished, he fell asleep in Jesus,
strong in the faith of our ultimate success. In
his death, this church lost a faithful laborer, an
exemplary Christian, and an efficient deacon. ·

We aimed, so far as it was practicable, to reach
all the members of the church. Many were at a
far distance. Some were in California, but generously came to our help. Deacon Westward F.
Keeling gave or collected one hundred dollars;
and deacon Robert Ruffin, then residing in Bur-
lington, N. J., and Sister Alvira Carter, in California, contributed fifty dollars each. Indeed, I
believe that it may be said in truth, that the
members generally gave according to their ability.
With the exception of about seventy dollars, fifty-
five of which I obtained from the First African
Baptist Church, in Richmond, Va., and about
twelve from the Gilfield Church, Petersburg, Va.,

and the other cases already named, the whole amount was raised in Philadelphia.

When the year had expired within one day, although I believed that I had used all the means possible within my reach, I lacked sixty or seventy dollars to make the subscription complete. I was perplexed, and knew not what to do. The year was about to close upon me; and, unless the deficiency was provided for, the subscribers would not be bound to pay the sums affixed to their names. Ascertaining, in the afternoon of that day, that there would be preaching in the evening, in the first Baptist Church, West Philadelphia, I sought the residence of brother Levy, the pastor, about an hour previous to the commencement of the service. I stated to him my difficulty, and requested permission to make an appeal to his people after the sermon. He replied that, if I would preach for him, I might tell my own story. I therefore preached a short discourse, and then presented my case. In fifteen minutes, the amount required was raised. And so ended my year's labor.

I then commenced to collect the amount subscribed, which I found to be the most difficult part of the work. This consumed the greater

9 I

part of another year. In consequence of change of circumstances, deaths, removals, and other causes, the collection of the whole subscription was rendered impossible. About twenty-seven hundred dollars were realized, which placed us in comparatively easy circumstances. It was not long before we succeeded in raising the balance due on the mortgage. Then we were free, with the exception of one hundred and sixty dollars ground rent. Previous to our first payment upon the mortgage, our current expenses amounted to about one thousand dollars per year. The interest on mortgage was three hundred dollars; pastor's salary four hundred; ground rent, one hundred and sixty; sexton, fuel, lights, &c., one hundred and forty-six—making, in all, one thousand and six dollars per annum. The amount of principal paid on our mortgage reduced the interest to one hundred and eighty dollars per year, bringing our annual current expenses about nine hundred dollars. This continued for about seven years. I apprehend that few of our colored churches ever had more formidable pecuniary difficulties to contend against, and succeeded. This, however, was not without its advantages to us. It was a trial of our faith, and a good opportunity was afforded

us to place all our trust in the Lord, so that when
we received help we knew from whence it came.
Thus it is that our heavenly Father helps those
who cannot help themselves, but seek help from
Him.

Our colored brethren are laboring under a gross
mistake in their theory of collecting money for
the payment of church debts. They assume that
it can be best done abroad. Not so. If prudence
has been exercised, the denomination interested,
and their confidence secured, it is better and more
easily done at home; and where this cannot be
done, it is usually best not to be attempted abroad.
I suppose my reception in England was as kind
and cordial as has been extended to any man in
similar circumstances; but yet I was obliged to
travel nearly all over that country at an expense
of between seven and eight hundred dollars, the
church meanwhile being deprived for nearly two
years of the services of a pastor, and his family of
a head, to collect about the same amount as was
subsequently realized in our own city. I hope
ever to remember with gratitude the kindness and
generosity of our brethren in Great Britain to the
church which I represented, and to our colored
brethren generally: but I found that which I was

slow to believe, and do most freely confess, that our friends at home, when once aroused to see the importance of the object, are not less generous in contributing to the necessities of the colored people than our friends abroad. "I have learned by experience," and therefore suggest to all my brethren who anticipate seeking foreign aid for any cause of Christian benevolence, to do so only as a last resort, and even then not without you are able to make out a very strong case; and when that is done, begin and work at home, not think of running all over the country to collect a few hundred dollars. Seek it in the vicinity where you are located, and I believe it will generally be obtained.

CHAPTER XXII.

PECUNIARY DIFFICULTIES—CHURCH EDIFICE IN THE HANDS OF THE SHERIFF—REMARKS ON THE DISPOSITION OF PROPERTY.

THE reader is requested to go back with me a little in my narration, that we may note some other facts of interest. The time spent in the operation of procuring subscribers and collecting the money was about two years. Those were years of care and anxiety. Some of our creditors became very impatient, and began to enforce their claims. Then all manner of rumors were circulated. It was predicted that our flourishing of trumpets amounted to nothing, and our apparent success would prove to be a failure. During those two years, the Sheriff's bill was placed upon the house twice. On each occasion, it appeared on the Saturday night. This, I doubt not, was designed to injure us. On one Saturday evening during this eventful period, deacon Williams came into my room in the rear of the church, evidently laboring under much excitement, and informed me

197

that the Sheriff's bill was on the house. Going
out with him, I observed quite a number of people
occupied in reading it. The rumor rapidly spread
that the meeting-house of the Shiloh Church was
certainly to be sold at Sheriff's sale. We then
consulted together as to the best course to be pursued. I told deacon Williams that he must either
borrow the money for six or nine months, or fur-
nish it himself. To this he interposed objections,
concluding by saying that to do either was impossible. I still insisted that under the circumstances,
with his influence with moneyed men, and his
knowledge of business, it was his duty to render
help in so pressing an emergency. He still per-
sisted in his refusal. Then, after telling him that
the money must be forthcoming, and the proceedings stopped, I requested him to take down the
bill, and procure some water to wash the place
where it had been posted.

This done, I resumed my work of making preparation for the Sabbath, almost assured that I
should have a large congregation. The morning
came, and the people began to rally unusually
early. Many inquiries were made for the Sheriff's
bill, the very existence of which, some having no
knowledge of the matter, they positively denied.

Others were anxious to ascertain the truth or falsity of the report; but, seeing deacon Williams and myself apparently unmoved, they concluded that it could only be a false rumor. I preached as well as I could under such trying circumstances, probably in some respects better than I should have done had I been free from so heavy a burden on my mind.

Early on Monday morning, I called upon a friend, related to him our difficulties, and requested his assistance, when he readily consented to loan the amount required for twelve months. Thus did the Lord once more interpose on our behalf. After paying one thousand dollars, which was the balance of the mortgage, we were allowed quietly to pursue our course.

Believing that such things ought not to be, and would not be, if Christians performed their whole duty, I would offer some reflections upon the obligation which devolves upon members of churches, not only to give during life, as the Lord has prospered them, but also to remember the church of Christ in their last will and testament. I believe that in this respect many professors of religion are manifestly at fault. Only one member of our church ever left us a legacy, and nothing was realized from that.   I am fully aware that there are but few among us who have anything to leave, but there are some who may need to be reminded that a cause for which they can pray and labor whilst they live, is worthy to receive a posthumous gift from them.   I have known some who possessed quite an extensive property, to die without paying their dues to the church—much less did they leave a legacy for its benefit.   And I have lived to see many instances where the property of deceased professing Christians was quickly squandered away.   Two of these are noticeable as affording a warning, and teaching a lesson.   One of them happened in H——; the other near this city.

In the first case, the individual was worth some three or four thousand dollars.   When she knew that she was about to die, she sent for a gentlemen to draft her will, and informed him that she was about to leave most of her property to be divided between his children and a cousin of his.   He assured her that they did not need her money, as they would be well provided for, and suggested that there was a poor church of the same denomination as that to which she was attached, and two colored young men of much promise, that needed just such help as she was prepared to afford. She rejected the suggestion with the remark that, if she could not bestow her property according to her own pleasure, she would leave it to the benevolent institutions of the Presbyterian church.

The other case was that of a member of a Baptist church, with whom I was well acquainted, who was apparently one of the most zealous members of the church, excepting in the matter of giving, and died possessed of some ten or fifteen thousand dollars. The church of which she was a member was in debt for their house of worship; yet she even failed to make provision for her monthly assessments due the church. After making some small provision for her adopted child, she left a large portion of her estate to a wealthy gentleman who had the charge of her business, and claimed to be a strong friend to the negro, but *not one cent to the church.* In this way, she almost totally ignored certain parties who had a legal right to the property. That colored persons, either through their ignorance or prejudice, should be sometimes induced to make such a disposition of their effects, is not surprising; but that gentlemen of wealth, who stand upon their dignity, should stoop so low as to accept such legacies, and

9 *

even to assist in maturing such arrangements—to rob the poor and fatherless children, to deprive the orphan of his right—is "passing strange."

There are colored people who have yet to learn the worth of the apparent respect (for it is only in appearance) which they receive beyond many of their friends, who are equally respectable, although poorer. If purchased by money, it is but of little worth. When a boy, I remember hearing of a very respectable colored man, who was possessed of considerable property. This it was which made him respectable, for men the wide world over are so considered, if they have money, no matter by what means they may have obtained it. To use his own phrase, he was "at home" everywhere. He scarcely realized that he was a black man. He was induced to aid his friends by giving loans and becoming surety, until he lost all. Then he found out that he was a colored man. His name was David Norton. When his money was gone, he lost the respect of his friends. "They used," said he, on one occasion, "to call me *Mister* Norton, but now it is Old David."

"These are spots in your feasts of charity." The professing Christian world is, I fear, at fault. Many Christian men and women have yet to learn

that, if God has prospered them in worldly sub-
stance far beyond others—that when making a
distribution of their property, it is their duty to
remember the church for the progress of which
they have professedly toiled and prayed, so that,
whether living or dying, their property should be
the Lord's. They should adopt the language,
with reference to the subject, of the sweet singer
of Israel—"If I forget thee, O Jerusalem, let my
right hand forget her cunning; if I do not remember thee, let my tongue cleave to the roof of
my mouth; if I prefer not Jerusalem above my
chief joy." The amount which a Christian may
bequeath to the church of Christ is not of so
much importance as the fact that the gift helps to
prove an abiding love to the Saviour, and to show
his measure of faith in the ultimate success of the
Gospel. How can a Christian of property die in
peace, without thus proving anew his loyalty to
the kingdom of the Lord Jesus? Surely, this is
a subject which needs consideration. Friends of
the Saviour, "Remember Zion!"

I cannot better close this chapter than by an
appeal to those who may read these pages, and
may have something to dispose of for benevolent
purposes, living or dying, to help Shiloh to pay

off her gronnd rent, which is two thousand six
hundred and eighty dollars, and let them own
their property in fee simple. If a few benevolent
persons were to leave in their last will and testament any part of that sum, to be applied with
interest when the whole amount should be provided, I have no doubt it would be as acceptable
to God as most legacies which are made. O, that
the cause of Shiloh may still be remembered by
the friends of Jesus! that in the providence of
God I may be permitted to see that beautiful
place of worship owned by the church! I think
all will agree that I have labored long and hard
enough to behold it. May the good Lord incline
the hearts of some of his children to perform it!

CHAPTER XXIII.

SICKNESS AND DEATH OF MY DAUGHTER ELLEN—REFLEC-
TIONS—ANOTHER CHILD—SPECIAL INTEREST IN THE
CHURCH UNDER THE PREACHING OF REV. J. M. RICH-
ARDS—HAPPY RESULTS.

THE year 1855 was to me one of mingled grief and joy; but I can yet truly say that the Lord was good. Early in the spring, my only daughter, who had just completed her education, and had commenced to learn a trade, was taken sick with the bilious fever, and confined to her room for four or five weeks. Although I felt a deep anxiety for her, the assurances of the physician were such, that I did not regard her disease to be dangerous. Near the close of her sickness, how- ever, she was taken with violent bleeding at the nose, which the physician succeeded in checking. She then appeared to improve slightly. On Wednesday evening, the 21st of March, as I was about to leave my house for my weekly preaching engagement at our church, I entered her room to speak with her, when she requested that I would stay with her. To that I readily consented, although I did not suppose that she was any worse. On account of her extreme weakness, I refrained from much conversation. About ten o'clock, she commenced bleeding again quite rapidly, when I went immediately for my physician, whom I found to be at the time in attendance upon one of his neighbors. He offered me a prescription, and promised to call and see my daughter previous to his return home. I waited only for his directions, which he was in the act of giving me when a messenger arrived in haste, and informed me of the most painful of all news, that my Ellen was dying. In company with the physician, I hastened home with all speed; but I was *too late !* Before we reached the house,· my dear daughter had breathed her last, and her spirit had returned to God who gave it. So severe a shock I had never before experienced; but, although I could not speak, I felt that "the Lord gave, and the Lord hath taken away; blessed be the name of the Lord." Thus were many of our hopes disappointed and our expectations blasted. We had cherished the fond desire that she might be preserved to be a comfort and help to us in our declining years; but the Lord, in His wisdom, was pleased to take her away in the very

bloom of her youth, thus making our hearts deso-
late. She died at the age of eighteen years and
three months, and had been a member of the
church for eleven months. During all her sickness, she manifested entire resignation to the will
of her heavenly Father. Whilst she expressed a
desire to live on our account, if it was the Lord's
will, she was entirely submissive, and willing to
commit herself into His hands. I can truly say
that she was respected and beloved by all her
friends, by a large circle of whom she was much
lamented. The funeral services occurred on the
following Sabbath, when a very interesting and
impressive discourse was delivered by my friend
and brother, the Rev. T. S. Malcom, from the text,
"Be ye also ready, for in such an hour as ye think
not the Son of man cometh." The church was
filled as it had not been since the day when she
was buried with Christ in baptism, and the congregation was deeply affected, I trust, to the everlasting profit of many.

Deep and sore as this affliction was, we were
comforted with the thought that our loss was her
eternal gain, and that therefore we could not sorrow as those who were without hope. This dispensation of the providence of God, dark and

incomprehensible as it appeared to be, has not, I hope, been without its especial benefit. I feel that it has taught me to sympathize the more with those who are similarly afflicted. Perhaps it was needful that I should drink such a bitter cup to the very dregs, for the ministers of Jesus Christ, of all other men, are most called to sympathize with the afflicted. This they can really do when a deluge of sorrow has rolled over their own souls. Then they are able to administer comfort and consolation as they themselves have been comforted of the Lord. This it is which will prepare them to bind up the wounded hearts of those who may have been called to mourn the loss of dear children or friends.

In August, we were blessed with our fifth and last child, which was a source of no small consolation to us—a comfort in the day of sorrow. We felt that the Lord sometimes removes one blessing that he may bestow another. Of the five children whom the Lord has given us, we have but two remaining, viz., Thomas Paul, born in Providence, R. I., in June, 1846, and John Isaiah, born in Philadelphia, in August, 1855. May the Lord give us wisdom and grace to educate them in His fear.

Nothing of special interest occurred in the church from 1855 to 1857. We lived in peace among ourselves, felt somewhat of the Spirit of the Lord to be with us, and enjoyed many profitable meetings. In February, 1857, the Rev. J. M. Richards kindly consented to labor with us in a protracted meeting. For two or three weeks, we met with but little encouragement. The vision tarried. Mr. Richards preached faithfully every night, and the brethren continued to wait on the Lord by prayer and supplication, until He poured down upon us His Spirit from on high, when commenced one of the most precious seasons of revival in which it has been my privilege to labor. On the third Sabbath in January, three willing converts were baptized. It was truly a refreshing time in Shiloh. The Word preached was attended with power from above. The congregations were large and attentive. From that time onwards, for some weeks, every day witnessed to a profession of faith in the Saviour by some souls; and on each successive Sabbath our house of worship was literally crowded by persons desirous of seeing the ancient rite administered, and happy souls rejoicing in the Lord.

Those meetings continued about eight weeks,

I 2

during which time great grace fell upon the people. It was indeed a period of deep interest to the church. Many will have occasion for everlasting gratitude to God that He ever sent brother Richards to labor with us. His success upon this occasion was no exception, for it pleases the Lord to bless his preaching in every part of the vineyard which he may visit, especially where religion has been at a low ebb, and brethren and sisters have become discouraged. His advent among them has always been like the coming of Titus. But the brother needs no letter of commendation from me. His praise is in all the churches. Nevertheless, I would recommend to the members of the poor and weak churches of Jesus Christ, when they feel to need help to move the ark of the Lord, to procure, if possible, the services of that man of God. And this for two reasons: 1st. They may confidently expect God's blessing to attend his labors, if they will exercise faith, and labor with him; and 2d. Because the Lord has so blessed him temporally, that Mr. Richards can afford to labor without the same amount of compensation which those of God's ministers ought to receive who have not been favored with a competency of this world's goods. He will be found to possess a willing heart and an ardent love for his Master's work.

As the result of this revival, about eighty were added to the church by baptism, and several others by letter and experience. Many of them have proved themselves valuable members of the church, some of which have died in the faith of the Gospel, and others like the dogs, returning to their vomit, and like the sow that is washed, to the wallowing in the mire.

CHAPTER XXIV.

SHILOH BAPTIST MEETING-HOUSE — LACK OF BENEVO-
LENCE—LIST OF CHURCHES—SELF-DENIAL OF THE
MINISTRY—ENCOURAGEMENTS TO LABOR—CONCLU-
SION.

FROM the time mentioned in the previous chapter unto the present, there has continued a good state of feeling in the church. There has been, also, quite a number of baptisms; but yet no special revival interest has been enjoyed. The most important transaction which has occurred among us was the repairing of our house of worship, which was commenced in the spring of 1860, and occupied seven months, at an expense of about fourteen hundred dollars. Those repairs, both within and without the building, were very thorough. Besides which, the building was enclosed by an iron fence. It is now not only the most substantial and commodious, but also the finest house of worship owned by our colored brethren in the denomination from Maine to Georgia, and east of the Rocky Mountains. It cost about twelve thousand dollars, including the ground. Although with a membership of about three hundred, and current expenses only seven hundred dollars per year, it might be supposed to be very easy to maintain it; yet it is not quite clear to my mind that the majority of the church have any just appreciation of the manner in which the Lord has favored us, and therefore not of their own true condition.   Perhaps no church ever had a more self-sacrificing, resolute, and determined set of members than are many of the Shiloh Church; but the majority are otherwise. The penurious and covetous spirit which maintains with many, I regard as one of the fruits of oppression, which it may take more than one generation to cure.

The system of slavery necessarily brings and keeps together a larger number of colored persons than would live in company under other circumstances.   If the people were free, they would naturally seek out those places which offered the best inducements to them for obtaining a livelihood.   Some would go to Africa, some to Hayti, whilst others in yet different directions.   We should not then see what now we are forced to behold in Richmond, Petersburg, Augusta, Savannah, and other places.

Take the following as an illustration: According to the census of 1850, the population of New York and Pennsylvania amounted in all to nearly six millions, with less than eighty thousand colored people. In Georgia and Virginia, there were about one million four hundred and seventy-four thousand; whilst the colored population, in those two States, numbered eight hundred and fifty-four thousand. My reason for selecting those two States is not because the colored population there is the largest, as the census shows that Kentucky and Tennessee far exceed them, but on account of the position of the Baptist interest in the two former States. The fact that the system of slavery binds our colored people together, and forces them so to remain, independent of their interests and their will, must be favorable to their securing large congregations. This must be especially seen when the fact is taken into consideration that matters connected with religion are the only subjects in which they are permitted any participation, and that, in many places, only on the Sabbath day. A person might appear to be a very good Christian in Richmond or Georgia, attending meeting on every Sabbath day, who, in Philadelphia or New York, would seldom attend public worship, and then reluctantly contribute anything to the cause. Or, if anything were given, it would be but a small sum, which, however, would be considered quite liberal in the South. Where two or three thousand persons are members of one church, how easy for such a membership to raise the one hundred or more dollars per quarter for the pastor's salary, which, in the South, amounts to about four or five hundred dollars per year. For this, however, few give more time to the church than to preach twice on the Sabbath, spending their time during the week in commerce, farming, or other secular occupations. If but half of the membership of such churches give but twenty-five cents each per month, or three dollars per year, there would always be a surplus in the treasury. But that will not be the case in the free States, where the congregations must necessarily be less, and the expenses greater. When, therefore, brethren remove from those densely populated regions and those overgrown associations, to settle where the colored people are much less numerous, and the churches more feeble, it will take some time to educate them to give according to their ability. My own experience with persons who were comparatively wealthy has confirmed me in that fact; although they might be, in every other respect, excellent Christians. If, therefore, our white brethren suppose that this class of persons to whom I refer can succeed, in the outset, in sustaining independent churches, I must pronounce them to be mistaken. The majority of our people need to be educated to give.

But very few persons have formed any adequate idea of the self-denial which a colored pastor must practice. I do not know of more than two colored churches that pay so much as $500 per annum, viz., the Independent Baptist Church, Boston, Mass., and the First Colored Church in Washington. The latter have also reduced theirs to $400 the last year.

There are only six churches, so far as my knowledge extends, which pay $400 per year for ministerial support, viz., the Abyssinian and Zion Baptist Churches, New York; the First African and Shiloh Churches, Philadelphia; the Second Church, New Bedford, Mass.; the Hamilton Street Church, Albany; and the Twelfth Church, Boston.

The Union Church, Philadelphia; Oak Street

Church, West Philadelphia; and Meeting Street Church, Providence, R. I., each pay an annual salary of $300.

In this enumeration, I may possibly have omitted two or three churches which should be added to the last classification; but I do not remember one that should be added to the first; although, doubtless, there are several of our churches fully able to pay the larger amount, and even more, were they willing to recognize their duty to make a sacrifice, and fully to believe the apostolic words, that "the laborer is worthy of his hire," and they that preach the Gospel shall live by the Gospel.

As an item of important interest, I will place on record, in this volume, a list of the colored Baptist churches which are associated together for the purpose of carrying on missionary operations, home and foreign. With reference to our foreign work, it may be desirable to notice that we have already commenced a mission in Waterloo, Sierra Leone, where we have sustained, for the past four years, our brother, William John Barnett, a native preacher, now in this country. He is supplying the Oak Street Baptist Church, West Philadelphia, being unable to return to his native land on

. 10 K

account of a deficiency in the treasury of the convention, produced by the stringency of the times. It is, however, confidently hoped and expected that sufficient means may soon be raised to forward him to his field of labor in Africa, in connection with another brother, to assist in the erection of a chapel, and more thoroughly to establish the mission generally.

The following is a list of the churches which have been connected with the Baptist Missionary Convention for a number of years:—

Abyssinian and Zion Churches, New York; First African, Shiloh, and Union Churches, Philadelphia; Oak Street Church, West Philadelphia; Twelfth and Independent Churches, Boston; Concord Street Church, Brooklyn; Third Church, Brooklyn, E. D.; First, Second, and Third (colored) Churches, Washington, D. C.; Union and Saratoga Street Churches, Baltimore; Meeting Street Church, Providence; Second Church, Geneva; Second Church, New Bedford; Hamilton Street Church, Albany; Shiloh Church, Newburgh; Pleasant Street Church, Nantucket; Berean Church, Carsville; Zion Church, New Haven; —— Baptist Church, Columbia; Third

Church, Rochester; Salem Church, New Bedford; and Michigan Street Church, Buffalo.

With one or two exceptions, it has been my privilege to visit and labor with each of the above-named churches, and I therefore claim to have had an opportunity to form some idea of their strength and the self-denial which their pastors are obliged to exercise in order to live comfortably, and be honest with all men. To show the necessity of self-sacrifice, let us take, for example, New York, Philadelphia, Boston, Baltimore, Washington, and other places of large population. It is but reasonable to suppose that the pastors of the churches in those cities would occupy a dwelling at a rental of about $150 per annum, which, in such places, would be considered a comparatively small rent. With such a deduction made from a salary of $400, only $250 remain for the clothing and general support of his family. Besides which, it is enjoined upon him to be "given to hospitality;" whilst, also, it is his duty to be liberal in his contributions to some of the Christian institutions of the day, that he may set before his brethren a proper example, and aid in forwarding the progress of the cause of Christ. It is, therefore, a hard problem to solve—how a minister of Christ, having a family, can live in a large city, where rent, fuel, and clothing generally command the highest prices, on so small a sum, without sometimes being subjected to sorer temptations than are likely to befall other men not engaged in the same calling. The natural solution of such a problem appears to be that he must either starve, enter upon some other pursuit in addition to his ministerial work (thereby neglecting many important duties pertaining to his high office), or contract debts which he sees no very certain prospect of liquidating. There does not seem to be any other alternative left to his choice. How can it be otherwise?

There is yet another pecuniary difficulty known to the colored pastor's experience, viz., scarcely one-half of the churches are punctual in their payments of even the small pittance promised. With this additional fact taken into consideration, it certainly cannot be very difficult to imagine the state of mind of that minister who has received a pledge from his brethren that his salary of three or four hundred dollars shall be punctually paid, yet, nevertheless, fail, until their indebtedness amounts to one hundred or one hundred and fifty dollars. One of my brethren in the ministry recently told me that the church was behind some three or four hundred dollars. Meanwhile, without regard to these facts, his church and congregation expect him to be industrious and faithful, and even as zealous as any other pastor in the vicinity, although very differently situated; and all this when he may feel himself to be under the dire necessity of going from house to house, for half of the day, seeking to obtain the favor of a small loan, to provide the commonest necessaries of subsistence for his family. Failing in that endeavor, he may then have recourse to his deacons, believing that they most certainly will give him aid and comfort. He relates to them his tale of sadness, enough to move a heart of stone, supposing it to be capable of receiving an impression from such a source. In reply, it is probable that he will be kindly told that the treasury is empty, and that, if the people fail in the payment of their subscriptions, the pastor, much to their regret, must wait patiently, especially as they hoped that an improvement would soon be effected. The deacons then promise to see the trustees, to whom the pastor, also, has recourse, as a last resort, and probably with the same result as in the former case. After spending one-half of the week, perhaps, in

thus seeking bread for his family, it is still expected that he will feed his flock with the good
Word of Life. But will the reader attempt to
imagine the character of sermons which a minister, with such a burden on his mind, would be
likely to preach. In addition to the expectation
of profitable sermons to be realized every Sabbath, the pastor must know, as if by common
instinct, of the sickness of every member of the
church—even of those who but rarely attend.
In short, he must preach and pray, visit the sick,
seek out the backslider, comfort the dying, administer the last offices to the dead, omitting no ministerial duty whatever; whilst his family are
craving bread, and his soul is in great distress. I
venture to assert that many of our colored ministers labor under such or similar disadvantages,
from year to year, until, at length, broken down,
they are brought to a premature grave, with their
ministerial character destroyed, because they could
not effect the impossibility of paying their debts
without means, any more than the children of
Israel could make bricks without straw.

The question may, perhaps, be asked, and with
some show of reason, If all this be true in fact,
why do not the colored ministers abandon the

profession, and enter upon some more lucrative
employment? To this it is replied that, having
received the Master's call and commission, we
endure the cross, and despise the shame for the
joy which is set before us, having full faith in the
promises of God. That faith enables us to persevere amid evil report and good report; whilst, in
the midst of all our trials, the Holy Spirit is oft-
times pleased to make us the humble agents of
effecting more good than if we dressed in fine
linen, rode in carriages, and fared sumptuously
every day. By reference to the minutes of the va-
rious associations with which some of the despised
colored churches are connected, it may be seen that
their poor pastors have been honored of the Lord
with as great, and sometimes with more abundant
success than many brethren who have been favored with an abundance of this world's sub-
stance.

But again: it may be inquired, Do not these
ministers receive many presents from their
churches and others, and are they not thus materially assisted? To this query I reply that, in
this respect, I presume I have been favored as
much as most of my colored brethren—even if
not more. My ministerial life now numbers

twenty-two years, twelve of which have been spent in Philadelphia, where there are about twenty Baptist churches, in all of which, during my residence in the city, pastoral changes have been made, excepting in the Tenth (Dr. Kennard's) and Shiloh Churches. Through all my career in the ministry, it has pleased the Lord (and I speak it to the praise and glory of His great name) to raise up friends, both in and out of the church, in Providence and Philadelphia, especially in the latter city, where my residence has been more protracted. During the twenty-two years of my ministry, I have received only five suits of clothes, with other smaller gifts; but still I have been able to make a respectable appearance. In Philadelphia, I have found many noble-hearted friends (the names of whom I would cheerfully mention, but I know it would be repugnant to their feelings), for whose unostentatious kindness I continue to feel most heartfelt gratitude, and to pray our heavenly Father to return their beneficence a thousand-fold into their bosoms.

> "Their works of piety and love,
>   Performed through Christ, their Lord,
>   Forever registered above,
>   Shall meet a sure reward."

I can have no doubt but that I am fully able to speak of the wants and self-denial of my brethren in the ministry; for, if the church with which it has been my privilege to labor for the past twelve years cannot adequately support their pastor, it is idle to talk of the ability of others. I know of no church, and I am acquainted with nearly all of our churches in the country, that enjoys the services of better officers. The deacons are good men, enjoying the respect of their brethren and sisters, and of the congregation generally; and I can have no doubt but that, under the direction of the Holy Spirit, and the labors of a faithful and judicious ministry, the church will ultimately succeed in establishing that system and uniformity so much needed in all of our churches, in order to the development of their strength, and growth in grace, and the prosecution of those works which advance the Redeemer's kingdom among men.

· And now, dear reader, we are brought to "the conclusion of the whole matter." I did not undertake this work because I vainly thought that I was better qualified for such a task than others of my brethren who are possessed of superior
10*

advantages and material to write their biographies, but mainly because that no Baptist minister of my own color, born out of bondage (so far as I am aware), has ever performed the work. There are some, however, which have been written by brethren who were once "slaves," whose books contain more romantic incidents, and which are doing much good by way of showing to the church and the world the operations of the system of slavery. Among those are the biographies of the Rev. Noah Davis, of Baltimore, and the Rev. Israel Campbell. "My Life in Bondage and my Life in Freedom," by the latter, is a most excellent work of that description, and will, I doubt not, receive, as it deserves, a large circulation. But these, although valuable as means to the end in view, are not of the description of books most needed to to assist in transmitting a history of our colored churches. What appears to be most needed in the present day are historical and biographical facts, touching the trials, successes, and management of ministers and churches in building up the kingdom of the Lord, the manifestation of God's grace to us, when engaged in the performance of the work which He has given us to do, that He may be glorified, and that thus the hearts of

brethren who may now be struggling with embarrassment, and are ready to faint, may be encouraged to put all their trust in the Lord of hosts,
and not to shrink back because there is a lion in
the way. I desire that brethren who come after
us may learn, from the experience of their prede-
cessors, that success will be insured in proportion
as they "attempt great things for God," exercising
faith in that divine strength which is sufficient for
all things. Then will they persevere until the
great object of their faith is attained.

Should any of the above results follow the publication of this short narrative, I shall feel to be
amply compensated for my labor, and rejoice that
in any way the Lord should be pleased to bless
the humble efforts of one so unworthy a place in
the kingdom of grace as that to which, in His
good providence, I have been assigned, and
which, I trust, relying upon His aid, ever to
magnify. And now to the Triune God be Praise,
Power, and Dominion, for ever and ever, world
without end. Amen.